THE
ASSISTANT

USA TODAY BESTSELLING AUTHOR
MARNI MANN

Copyright © 2019 by Marni Mann
All rights reserved.

Visit my website at: www.MarniSMann.com
Cover Designer: Hang Le, By Hang Le, www.byhangle.com
Editor: Jovana Shirley, Unforeseen Editing, www.unforeseenediting.com
Proofreader: Judy Zweifel, Judy's Proofreading, and Kaitie Reister

No part of this book may be reproduced or transmitted in any form or by any means, electronic or mechanical, including photocopying, recording, or by any information storage and retrieval system without the written permission of the author, except for the use of brief quotations in a book review.

This book is a work of fiction. Names, characters, places, and incidents either are products of the author's imagination or are used fictitiously. Any resemblance to actual persons, living or dead, events, or locales is entirely coincidental.

For Stacey Jacovina, my warrior.

PLAYLIST

"Unsteady"—X Ambassadors
"Hurts Like Hell"—Fleurie
"Is There Somewhere"—Halsey
"Hemorrhage (In My Hands)"—Fuel
"Until We Go Down"—Ruelle
"Bruises"—Lewis Capaldi
"Too Good at Goodbyes"—Sam Smith
"Don't Hold Me"—Sandro Cavazza
"Trouble"—Halsey
"Lovely"—Billie Eilish with Khalid
"The Other Side"—Ruelle
"Even If It Hurts"—Sam Tinnesz
"Soldier"—Fleurie

PROLOGUE

JESSE - TWO MONTHS AGO

"I'M HERE," I whispered to my father, taking a seat next to his bed, moving the chair as close to him as I could.

Never taking my eyes off his face, I searched for his hand on top of the blanket and wrapped my fingers around it. His skin was so rough and dry. It felt nothing like the hand I'd held when I was a child or the one that had walked me down the aisle or the one I'd clung to hours after giving birth to my daughter.

My father had been there for everything.

And, soon ... he wouldn't be.

My lids squeezed tightly together, fat tears dripping past them, rolling down each cheek. I just wanted a moment without all the beeping from the heart monitor and humming of the ventilator, without the constant smell of alcohol and bleach and antibacterial gel.

That was impossible now.

With all the time I'd spent in this hospital, I should have

been used to the sounds and smells. I should have been able to block them out.

I couldn't.

Even when I wasn't here, I heard the noises of his room. I saw the starkness of the walls and felt the coldness on my skin. The same thing happened every time I closed my eyes and whenever I thought about tomorrow.

But there was one thing I didn't hear. The sound of my father's voice. From him, I got complete silence. I just wished he would say my name one last time, so I could soak the syllables into my memory.

I wanted to hold on to them the same way I was grasping his hand.

It was a wish that would never be granted.

So, what I had to do was listen to his eyes. They had been his voice for a while, and they'd been telling me how tired he was getting, how much pain he was in, how he couldn't take any more.

He wanted it to be over.

But he was worried about my mom. He loved her with everything he had. He'd been fighting to stay here with her.

It had been the hardest eight-year battle I'd ever witnessed.

I looked down at his long fingers. His nails were cut perfectly, filed until round, and cuticles trimmed. Hands so clean, they always smelled like soap. They still did even though he'd been in the hospital for weeks. She took care of him, no matter where he was.

I'd learned so much from her.

"Dad," I started, gazing back up to meet eyes the same color as mine, "we'll take care of Mom. You don't have to worry about her."

She was right outside the door. She wanted to give me a few moments alone with him, but she wouldn't go far.

"She will have everything she'll ever need and more. Dad ..." My voice broke as I waited for him to squeeze back. To blink. To acknowledge I was even speaking.

It was far too late for that.

I just ... hoped.

My cheeks were suddenly burning, the fire getting worse with every tear that streamed down. The air was getting thicker, making it more difficult to breathe. My heart was racing so fast; my body shook.

I have to get out of here.

That was the only thought in my head, followed by a feeling I'd never felt before. It was a rottenness in the pit of my stomach, aching so badly that it forced me to my feet.

I leaned over my father and pressed my lips to his forehead.

Oh God, this hurts.

"I love you, Daddy."

As I pulled my mouth away to gaze into his tired eyes, the urge to run became so overwhelmingly strong that I released his hand and whispered, "Bye, Dad," before I hurried into the hallway. I immediately saw my mother and said, "I'm going for a walk," as I passed her.

She knew how hard this was for me.

That was why she let me go, not saying a word as I wandered down the stairs and found myself three floors down in the cafeteria. My stomach churned from the smell. I wasn't sure what time it was or when I had last eaten. I couldn't even think about putting food in my mouth. But I needed something to soothe my stomach and to warm me since I was shivering.

I grabbed a tea and brought it into the elevator. I got off on my father's floor. I expected to go back into his room, take a seat next to my mother, and wait, my ears filled with beeping, my nose with rubbing alcohol.

The doctors had been telling us for four days that we were near the end.

I'd known we were approaching it for a while. He just kept fighting, but from what I could see, he wasn't going to for much longer.

When I approached his room, I learned that was a reality.

I didn't feel the tea that sloshed out of the top of the cup and burned my hand. Because, in that moment, all I felt was coldness. All I heard was the alarm on my father's heart monitor going off as he flatlined. The only thing I saw was the nurse hitting several buttons, and then the room turned silent —no ventilator, no beeping, no humming. She didn't grab the paddles or perform CPR.

He had a DNR.

As I walked in a little more, I should have been looking at my father, taking in his face, memorizing more of it even though I knew every line and freckle. I should have been standing at his side, holding his hand.

I wasn't doing either of those things.

I was frozen halfway between the entrance and the bed, staring at my mother, watching her expression.

My father had once told me it was easy to determine how much a man loved his soon-to-be wife on their wedding day. You had to watch the groom as the bride walked down the aisle, and his face would give him away.

What I learned in those few seconds was watching someone die was no different.

And it was that look—the one my mother had on her face right now—that would haunt me for the rest of my life.

ONE
JESSE
AFTER

"THIS IS the hardest thing I've ever done," I said, staring into the eyes of my executive team.

Some sitting at this table were the very first employees I'd hired when I started Cinched, a company that designed and manufactured shapewear, nineteen years ago at the age of twenty-three. Out of that group, a select few knew the news I was about to deliver. Others had speculated, I was sure. Over the last five months, I'd laid the groundwork, gradually spending more time out of the office than in it, getting it ready to operate without me. The business was healthy. The last thing I needed was to create waves.

"What I learned from my dad"—I took a breath, trying to find a voice that wasn't full of emotion. I'd told myself I wasn't going to cry today, and I meant it—"was a little something about time." My voice softened. "How precious and valuable it is." I paused again. I'd rehearsed this speech for weeks. It had sounded so much better in my head. "And, right now, my time needs to be spent with my family." I swallowed, the back of my throat pulsing, preparing myself for the news I had to deliver. "It's time I take a large step back and let you all run the show. I'll still be involved but from afar, and I won't be part of the day-to-day."

I remembered when my high school drama teacher had taught us how to cry on demand. We were told to concentrate on something so incredibly sad until the emotion overtook us. After several tries, I'd mastered it. What I had become even better at was holding in the tears, and this moment was really testing that.

Cinched was my first baby, making it a sensitive topic. So was knowing I'd reached the point in my life when I had to pull away and focus on my family.

My emotions were stirring.

They had been since I made the decision.

I looked at my vice president of sales, remembering his wedding ten years ago in Boston. It had been summer and outdoors, and I had danced under the stars.

I took a breath and said, "I've watched this team tackle hurdles I wasn't sure the company would ever overcome, some so large that they threatened to put us under. You didn't let that happen. You worked, you sacrificed, and you exceeded every sales objective I'd ever set. I don't have to tell you to take care of Cinched because I know you will."

Several moments of silence passed before my CFO broke it and said, "On behalf of everyone at Cinched, I can say I'm going to miss seeing you every day. It's a good thing I know where to find you when I need a Jesse fix."

I'd known her the longest and worked with her the closest.

When she'd first started, I couldn't afford an office, so she'd come to my tiny apartment, and we'd worked on laptops at my kitchen table. By the end of those two years, I could order for her off a menu and dress her every morning. When she had gone into labor with her first child, it'd happened in my office. I'd driven her to the hospital and sat with her in the delivery room until her husband arrived.

"Thank you," I whispered to her and then quickly glanced away, looking at the foreheads of the other team members. That was easier than connecting with their eyes. The sharp reality of not walking in here on Monday morning was suddenly becoming more real by the second.

I made the mistake of gazing down, seeing my director of marketing. She had now been in remission for two years. We celebrated after every round of chemo. Some of those celebrations took place on her couch, but we still acknowledged every one. She had fought so hard, and she was still here, stronger than ever.

I forced myself to glance away, and I met more eyes, more history staring back at me. Pasts that were so incredibly thick.

I didn't need to say good-bye or shake their hands or hug them. I wasn't leaving. I was backing up. There was a huge difference.

I released the edge of the table, a slab of oak I'd been squeezing since I sat down, and I offered them all a smile. "Thank you for giving me the best years of my life." My hand then went into the air, and I waved for a few seconds before I walked out of the conference room.

I stopped in my office just long enough to grab my coat and purse, and then I immediately headed to my car. The cold made the door creak as I climbed in the driver's seat. My hand shook as I pressed the button that started the engine. I didn't turn on the radio. I just pulled out of the parking lot in complete silence and drove through downtown Burlington, Vermont, on this blistering February day. Ice sparkled on my windshield. Snow crunched under my tires. I could focus on these sounds rather than replaying the last several minutes in my head.

There were the words I had said, and then there were the ones that never got past my tongue.

They were nothing alike.

At the stoplight, I could turn left, and I would be home in four minutes. Instead, I went right, heading toward Saint Michael's College where I'd been spending most of my afternoons. Six miles later, I was at the entrance of the campus, weaving my way through its narrow streets.

I parked directly in front of the library, grabbed the small bag from the backseat, and hurried inside to get out of the cold.

"Jesse," I heard as I stepped past the doorway, just starting to loosen my scarf.

I scanned the open space around the entrance until I found the source of the voice.

My friend Bay was standing by the first row of books, holding several folders against her chest, smiling at me.

"Hi," I said once I made my way over to her. I pulled her in for a hug, squeezing for several beats before I let her go. When I did, I held out my hand with the bag. "This is for you."

Her cheeks reddened. I could tell she was genuinely surprised. "You bought me something?"

"I saw it in the window of a store, and it reminded me of you."

"Jesse ..." I could see the appreciation in Bay's eyes. It was a beautiful thing. "You really shouldn't have."

"It's just something small." I nodded toward the bag. "Open it."

She moved over to a nearby table and set the bag on top, reaching inside to remove the box. There was a red bow taped to the top that the salesclerk had insisted on. Bay lifted it off along with the lid, and the largest grin came across her face. "Oh, Jesse, I love it."

It was a keychain, and dangling from it was a lemon made entirely of yellow crystals. It wasn't large or flashy—things she wouldn't like. It was petite and understated, like her.

She held the keychain in her palm and closed her fingers around it, bringing it up to her heart. "I'll cherish it. Forever."

If I hadn't cried at my office, I certainly wasn't going to here, but Bay was making that so difficult.

I pointed toward the back of the library. "I'm going to go. You know where I'll be."

"Studying today?" she asked before I moved.

I shook my head and took a breath. It hurt during the inhale. It hurt even worse when I exhaled. "I'm going to catch up with an old friend."

"An old ..." Her voice trailed off as she thought of who I was talking about. Once she figured it out, she laughed. It was a sound I needed to hear today. "Go enjoy yourself, Jesse."

Without saying a word, just giving her a slight nod, I turned and walked away. I wasn't more than a few paces from her when she spoke my name again.

As our eyes connected, she mouthed, *Thank you.*

I smiled, holding our stare for several seconds before I continued moving toward the back of the library, finally reaching my favorite shelf. These hardcovers had spines that were as dark and cracked and weathered as the ones I had at home. Time had changed the outside, but the inside was untouched and timeless.

That made me love them even more.

I lifted *Macbeth* off the shelf, opened it somewhere in the middle, and inhaled. The musky scent of paper and dust and age filled my nose. Certain scents brought back so many memories. This one was of my father.

I carried the book over to one of the large leather chairs and took a seat, my eyes gradually falling onto the page.

I had four hours ...

To escape.

I opened the garage to our house and drove in, turning off my car and going right inside. I only made it as far as the powder room before I heard voices.

They were sounds I loved more than anything in this world.

"Tommy," my daughter, Viv, said to my son, "don't you remember that, in order to calculate the area inside the compound shape, you have to ..."

I didn't stop walking until I reached a spot in the family room where I could see my two children sitting at the island in the kitchen. Tommy had several notebooks and books spread out in front of him. Viv held a pen and was pointing to something on one of the pages.

At first, I hadn't been sold on the idea of Viv helping Tommy with his math homework, and I'd thought a private tutor should be brought in. My son was struggling with the subject, and I quickly assumed a professional would be a better route. But Viv excelled in math. She had offered, and Tommy was comfortable with it. So far, the arrangement was working out really well.

My two kids couldn't be any more different.

Viv, my seventeen-year-old, was fierce, independent, and extremely determined—the way I'd raised her to be. She wanted to be an architect, like her father, and was going to MIT next fall. She would join her dad's firm once she graduated college. Boys were really starting to give my beautiful daughter attention, and she was learning how to balance that along with her senior year of high school, her friends, and her studies, all while not caving from the expectations we set for her.

She had something to prove ... and she would.

"*Ughhh*," Tommy groaned, tapping his finger on the notebook. "I just don't get it."

My twelve-year-old was just like me. Creative, unable to wrap his head around an equation, preferring to make something with his hands or his words. We babied him a little more than Viv. He needed it. But, where Viv's drive came from her need to succeed, Tommy's was led by emotion.

He was the one I worried about the most.

There was movement in the back of the kitchen, and my eyes slowly connected with Emery's. A smile bigger than I'd worn all day came across my face. Twenty-four years. That was how long I'd been with that man.

There was a sensation in my stomach, a fluttering on the inside of my navel. It happened every time I saw him.

Still.

I looked at my little family, and in that moment, I knew I was doing the right thing.

They needed me.

And, boy, did I need them.

I finally stepped forward, and Tommy called out, "Hi, Mom," when I approached him.

I pressed my lips to the top of his head. The scent of a twelve-year-old boy was about as stale as the gym clothes he always forgot to bring home from school. It didn't matter. I loved every bit of that kid.

"Hi, baby," I said into his hair.

Then, I moved to Viv, kissing the side of her forehead, leaving my lips there so that I could breathe her in. I could smell the orange she'd eaten when she got home from school and the new shampoo I'd picked up for her last week. "Thank you for helping your brother."

"Sure, Mom."

I turned and walked toward my husband, my arms wrapping around his neck, my body pressing against his. "How was your day?"

He bent his head down and gave me the softest kiss. "I got it."

My entire body tensed until I pulled away and saw that his expression confirmed what I'd thought. "Oh my God," I said, throwing my arms around him once more. "Emery, you did it."

A new high-rise was going to be built in the Back Bay of Boston. The builder had requested bids from architects located all over the world, and my husband had been chosen.

This wasn't just an honor. This was life-changing.

And it couldn't have happened at a better time.

I cuddled into his neck, clutching him with all my strength. "I'm so proud of you."

"You know what this means ..." His tone took away some of the excitement. "Two nights a week," he added before I had a chance to respond. "Three, max."

Emery and I had met our freshman year at Northeastern and lived together in the city after we graduated. It was too expensive to start a business there, so when I'd opened Cinched, we'd relocated to Burlington. About five years ago, we'd purchased a brownstone in the Back Bay, and we still took the kids there at least one weekend a month.

Boston wasn't the issue. It was how much time he'd be spending away from his family.

It was my job to worry about things like this.

Not his.

I leaned back to show him my eyes, knowing he needed the reassurance. "Listen to me; it's all going to work out just fine."

His stare didn't lighten, even when he said, "This is a decision I want us to make together."

I kept my voice low, so the kids wouldn't hear, and I clung to his leather belt. "We made it when you submitted your design. I knew back then what it would mean if you got the project." I smiled. "My feelings haven't changed, Emery. I'm so, so thrilled for you."

He cupped my face and dragged me closer for a kiss. "I don't know what I would do without you."

A few seconds after his lips left mine was when I finally opened my eyes, immediately getting greeted with the question, "How was your day, baby?"

My day.

An eruption of emotion happened all at once, and I did

everything I could to shove it away, making sure nothing showed on my face. I wasn't ready to talk about it. I needed a night—at least.

So, I stared into my husband's honest, loyal, intoxicating gaze. I put on a smile. And I lied, "It was perfect."

TWO
JESSE
AFTER

WHEN EMERY HAD DESIGNED and built our house, he'd made the back of our master bedroom an entire wall of windows. There were eight massive panes of glass, all of them uncovered. He didn't want anything hindering the view of the mountains or the two acres of forest in between. That meant, from the moment the sun rose to the second it set, our room was filled with light. Normally, I was out of bed before the rays touched my face. But, today, I felt their warmth heating my skin, and I saw it sparkling over the fluffy white comforter. Every few seconds, the glimmering fabric would shift, movement originating from between my legs.

That was where Emery's mouth was.

"*Ahhh*," I moaned, bending my knees while I gripped the fabric beneath me. I drove the top of my head into the pillow as a sensation began to build in my core. My chest heaved from the intensity of it. I rocked my hips forward once the tingling shot through my navel and went straight up to my breasts. "Emery!"

He licked past each wave of pleasure, his fingers circling within me, causing the quietest scream to empty from my lips.

I couldn't let the kids hear me.

But I couldn't hold it in either.

I tilted my head forward just in time to see the blanket fall past his neck, finally revealing my husband's face. Our eyes connected as the final shudder ripped through my body.

"Emery," I said once more, this time much softer and this time with the last bit of energy I had left.

He flattened his tongue, swiping it slower, and I breathed out a final sigh. Then, I released the sheet and straightened my knees, my body fully pressed against the bed.

Where I remained still, Emery moved to the spot next to me, wrapped an arm across my navel, and rested his chin on my shoulder. "I wish I could do that every morning."

He still looked at me as though I were eighteen, the age when we'd met. As though I hadn't bore two children. As though I were the sexiest woman in the world despite designing shapewear that kept me sucked in. As though his mouth on my body was how he genuinely wanted to start every day.

Most of my girlfriends complained about having too much sex with their husbands, acting like it was a chore. I was the opposite. Emery and I always had a healthy sex life, and the kids never got in the way of that.

I extended my arm, brushing my fingers through his hair.

How did I get so lucky?

As my fingers squeezed a section of his locks, I remembered I still hadn't told him my news. It had been a whole forty-eight hours since I informed my team, and I hadn't breathed a word of it to him.

It was too hard.

But it was time.

Fortunately, I'd stumbled upon the perfect way to introduce it. "You can," I said softly into his face.

I moved my hand to his cheek just as he said, "I can't get up at five to catch you before your run. I hate early mornings; you know that."

My fingers twitched as each of his words vibrated against my skin.

My run.

I pushed that thought aside.

"That's not what I'm suggesting," I told him.

"What's your idea then?"

I waited until I knew my voice would be completely steady before I said, "I stepped back from Cinched."

He pulled away from my shoulder to get a better view of me, his stare moving between my eyes. So many different emotions crossed his face. "When?"

"Friday."

"Jesse, why didn't you tell me?" His tone told me he was hurt, and that was understandable. We told each other everything.

We used to ... at least.

"I needed a minute to process, Emery. This was a big decision for me to make, and I've been extremely torn up about it." Tears were filling my eyes, but I wouldn't let them fall. "Since Dad ..." And then I stopped, unable to finish the sentence.

"I get it, baby." He sat up higher, his hand rubbing across my navel. "After losing your dad, you want to be with your family instead of spending eighty hours a week at the office."

I nodded.

"You know I've wanted you to trim your workload for a while, so I'm really happy about this." His lids narrowed, and I could tell he wasn't done speaking. "But, if you were thinking about pulling back, I just don't understand why you didn't talk to me about it."

I took a breath, hating how hard it was to do that. "I didn't want you to influence my decision. I wanted this move to be completely on me."

He didn't speak for several seconds, and then, with a gentle voice, he said, "I finally have you home." His hand was now on my face, cupping my cheek. "What's this going to look like?"

I nuzzled into his hold, grateful for what he'd asked, as it was another topic I hadn't been sure how to approach. "I don't want to come home and suddenly be busier than when I worked full-time. I want more time with my kids. I want more time for us."

He gripped me tighter as though he needed to emphasize his words as he said, "I want that, too."

"Then, Emery, I think you need to hire an assistant. Because, by being home, I worry that person will turn into me."

For years, he hadn't wanted an assistant in our house. He had a team of designers who worked remotely and an accountant who did all his bookkeeping. He had no one to help him with the daily responsibilities even though he desperately needed it.

"I can see that happening," he admitted.

I flattened my fingers against his arm and slowly moved them up to his chest. I loved how the short hairs felt against my skin. "If you're going to be focused on Boston now, which is what you should be doing, you will need someone maintaining your day-to-day work and your other projects and someone who can travel and assist you while you're in the city."

I saw him consider the pros and cons and calculate a salary that we wouldn't even notice was missing from our account.

"I think you're right," he said. "It's time I hire one."

I pressed my lips against his. Just once and only for a second but kissing him as though I were rewarding him.

"I have one favor to ask," he added.

"Okay."

"Do you mind running the employment ad and vetting the applicants? And maybe sitting in on the interviews? You have a knack for picking the right team members, and I need you to really weigh in heavily when choosing mine because they're going to be working in our home and traveling with me."

I put my hand on his face, my thumb skimming across his lip. Sometimes, he made things so easy for me, and I loved him for it.

"I'd be happy to."

His smile told me he was satisfied with my answer, and he began to move again, this time lowering on top of me, his mouth going to my shoulder, his dick slowly sliding between my legs.

He was hard.

That wasn't a shock.

While he kissed across my neck, I quickly thought about the verbiage I would send him tomorrow for the ad I was going to post. I'd written it when the idea for an assistant first came to me, but I needed his input for the specific tasks I might have missed in the description. Once the résumés started coming in,

I would reach out to four applicants and set up interviews for the following week.

Satisfied with the way things were turning out, I lifted my feet, my toes bending and tightening, to wrap my legs around Emery's waist, welcoming him inside me.

He teased but never entered, flirting with me when he said, "I can't believe you finally did it."

I didn't know why, but I felt the need to respond, turning the conversation more serious despite the fact that my husband was on top of me. "Viv will be going off to college next year. Tommy is months away from thinking we're the uncoolest parents on the planet. I missed so much of their childhood because of my job."

His mouth went to my forehead, and he held it there while he breathed against me, each exhale getting slightly deeper as his tip moved further in. "The kids are going to be so happy when they hear the news," he said.

My eyes closed, and a single tear dripped down my cheek. "I know." I wiped it away before he saw it, and when his eyes found me again, I moaned.

THREE
CHARLOTTE

UNTIL THIS MORNING, Charlotte didn't know what it felt like to wake up on a Monday and not have a job to drive to. It was purely out of habit that she had set her alarm the night before and gotten up at a quarter past six, the same time she'd been rising for the last three years. She then brought a mug of coffee into the shower, setting it next to her shampoo, sipping it as she began her regular routine. It wasn't until she stepped out of the warm spray that she realized she didn't have to dry her wet hair or dress in a conservative outfit or drive the short distance to work where she'd spend the next nine hours.

That was because, after deciding she needed to try something new, she had given her two-week notice, and she'd already completed her last day.

That didn't mean she was going to do nothing today. There were plenty of things in her apartment that needed to be cleaned and organized. But, before she dug into any of that, she twisted her sopping hair into a knot on top of her head, slipped on some comfortable clothes, and took a seat at her small desk. Once the monitor turned on, she typed in the web address of a local job search site and scanned through each of the listings.

Only one headline caught her attention.

Executive assistant to an architect, in-home work environment. Flexible schedule and traveling required.

Charlotte had been single for over a year and didn't have any children, which gave her the most flexible schedule. Traveling was something she would love to do. And, although she had never worked in someone's home, it was an environment she was sure she would enjoy.

She clicked the link, and a more detailed job description popped up. The bullet points said it was a full-time, salaried position. The trips would consist of flying back and forth between Burlington and Boston with several overnight stays every week. An extensive list outlined the administrative tasks. The last bullet point mentioned there would be two teenagers in the home, and light duties, involving cooking and transportation, could occur but wouldn't happen regularly.

Charlotte had worked jobs that were much more strenuous than the responsibilities she had just read, so she knew she could handle the position. Besides, administrative duties came easy to her, and she loved kids. Her sister was a single mom, and Charlotte had helped raise her two nieces since the day they were born.

But she didn't immediately click the Apply button. She stared at it, her finger hovering above the mouse, as she tried to make sense of all the different thoughts in her head. She knew her life was in the process of changing in so many ways, and it would be a long time before anything felt normal again. She also knew this was only the first step in achieving what she was after.

She told herself she was ready for it as the screen came back into focus, and her finger fell onto the mouse. She followed the instructions to upload her résumé, and once the confirmation appeared, Charlotte got up from the chair and went over to her closet, looking at every piece of clothing that hung on the rack. Because of the jobs she'd had in the past, everything she owned was so traditional—solid colors, high necks, and fitted skirts. She had very little fun clothes.

What was needed for an interview like this was something different than what she was looking at. What she needed was an outfit that showed her personality.

Closing her closet, she went over to the couch and lifted her phone off the coffee table, opening a popular shopping app. In less than fifteen minutes, she purchased eight shirts, four pairs of jeans, and three pairs of pants that would all be delivered to her doorstep in the next few days.

Efficient was one of the adjectives that had been used in the bullet points. Charlotte was pleased with how well she'd just proven that to be true.

She was even more pleased when an e-mail came in two days later, inviting her to Emery Black's house to interview for the executive assistant position. The time she was expected to arrive, his address, and a phone number were included.

Charlotte's hands shook with nerves as she replied to his e-mail, thanking him for the opportunity and confirming she would be there at the time he'd requested.

There was a lot of pressure to nail this interview.

Somehow, she had to get it right.

FOUR
JESSE
AFTER

EMERY OPENED my car door and held out his hand for me to grab. My fingers slipped across his palm, and I clasped his wrist, letting him pull me to my feet. Once I was outside, standing at the mouth of the Webbs' driveway, he led me closer to him, gripping me with one arm while his other carried a birthday gift.

"Thank you for coming tonight," he said.

The Webbs' house was less than twenty feet away. I could hear music coming from inside. I knew all the people in there, the owners of all these cars in the driveway, and how they'd greet us the second Emery and I walked through the door.

And that was part of the reason my stomach had been in knots all day.

This was the first time in five months that I was attending a party. Those had been the worst months because of my father, because of all the tests and treatments the doctor had been experimenting with.

When I was aching so badly on the inside, it was too difficult to smile with friends. I had a mask I was an expert at putting on that I wore for my family and colleagues. But, beyond that, I just didn't have it in me to go out and mingle.

Emery had been after me to respond to Alicia Webb's text, regarding her husband's forty-fifth birthday, which was taking place tonight at their home. I didn't want to go, but Emery gently pushed. With a softness in his voice, he reminded me it had been two months. He'd said it so sweetly again this morning and when we were getting into his car to come here. He must have thought I needed to hear that number over and over to feel better about this, as though there were a reasonable period of mourning and I had reached it.

Time wasn't something I had a problem keeping track of anymore. Emery just didn't understand that.

I glanced to my right and then the left, making sure we were alone before I said, "I'm not sure I'm ready for this." The air was so cold; it looked like smoke was coming from my lips.

Emery pressed into me even more, his wool jacket rubbing against mine. His exhales kept me warm, heating my face after each one. "These are our friends, Jess. They love you. They miss you. They miss us."

He was right.

The majority of the people in that house were our friends. They had sent food, they'd come to the funeral, and they'd extended invites even though I continuously declined.

That didn't make tonight any easier.

"Can we at least leave before eleven?" I slid my hands to the lapels of his coat.

It was eight now, but the party had started at seven. We were never normally late to anything. Had I wanted to be here, we would have been on time.

"You know the Roys will stay until at least two, and I'm sure the Foxes have hired a new nanny by now, so they probably won't even go home."

His thumbs pressed into the center of my cheeks, his lips wet from licking them. "Of course, baby." The lights shone across the driveway and lit up his face, showing how intensely he was staring at me. "But just try to enjoy yourself tonight." His eyes dropped to my mouth. "You look so beautiful."

I was covered in a jacket, and there was a scarf wrapped around my neck. He couldn't see what I looked like. Maybe that was the point, and he had intended to make me laugh.

I kissed him for trying, and as I pulled my mouth away, he said, "It's time."

I felt his fingers search for mine, and when they linked together, he began to lead me up the driveway, stopping on the last step to press the bell.

Several seconds passed before the door opened, and Alicia appeared. "Emery," she said, smiling at him, leaning in to kiss his cheek. Her grin turned sympathetic when she turned to me. "Oh, honey, get over here." I was suddenly in her arms, getting squeezed, while she whispered in my ear, "You know how sorry I am about your dad."

"Thank you," I replied.

My eyes connected with Emery's as he walked into the house, heading to the mancave where the husbands always hung out and played cards, drinking scotch and smoking cigars. The women would be in the kitchen where there was plenty of wine.

"Come on," Alicia said. "The girls are dying to see you."

Her hand clung to my arm, and I rushed behind her, still wearing my jacket as she pulled me through her house.

"Jesse, you're finally here," I heard the moment my feet hit the threshold of the kitchen.

I looked for the source, but there were at least ten women in here, which made it too many to tell.

"Hi, ladies," I replied, unwrapping my scarf and unbuttoning my jacket, setting both on a chair. Then, I moved over to the island.

"Red or white?" Alicia asked.

Before I had the chance to respond, someone wrapped their arms around me, hugging me so hard.

"Red," I called over the hugger's shoulder.

"Emery told Lee all the details," the hugger said.

Now that I'd heard her voice, I realized it was Karen, the wife of our attorney, whose home Emery had designed.

"I can't even imagine how hard that was to see. Or what it was like to go through that. Or how you are all healing from this."

"Thank you," I whispered as she pulled away.

It didn't matter how soft I spoke, everyone in this house had heard what my family had gone through. Burlington wasn't gossipy, but when it came to health, word traveled fast.

"How are you holding up?" Belle, a neighbor, asked.

The mask was on so tight that it was cutting off all my air, especially with having all of these eyes on me. The kitchen was silent as they waited for my response. I had to say something.

I looked at the glass of wine Alicia was pouring for me and shrugged. "I don't know, honestly."

Karen wrapped her arm around me. "That's understandable. You take as much time as you need. This isn't going to feel better overnight."

Alicia set the glass in front of me and said, "Jamie says you haven't been in the office much."

Jamie was Alicia's daughter, who was a senior at the University of Vermont, studying marketing and doing an internship at Cinched for the year. I'd been so preoccupied that I'd forgotten she was there and that she would have noticed my absence and reported it back to her mom.

Since that was the case, then there was a chance everyone in this house had already heard the latest news. If by chance they hadn't, then they were going to now.

"I pulled back from Cinched. With everything going on, it was just time."

"Of course it was," Alicia said, putting her hand on my arm while Karen tightened her grip on my shoulders. "When I lost my mom, I couldn't sleep. I'd just lie awake and think about her. Finally, I went to my doctor, and he had to put me on something because I couldn't function anymore. It was awful." Her fingers rubbed over my sweater, her thumb swiping back and forth like she was deleting e-mails. "My mom died in her sleep. But, if I had to watch her cling to life for as long as your dad did ..." Her eyes began to fill. "You haven't had it easy, honey."

I couldn't comment. I couldn't even agree. If I did, I'd fall apart, and that didn't need to happen in her kitchen. So, I focused on something that wouldn't make me cry and changed the conversation. "It's amazing how many closets I've neglected by working eighty hours a week." I tried to smile. I was sure it looked forced, but it was still on my lips. "I have lots to keep me busy."

"If you don't ever go back to Cinched, that's okay, too,"

another woman said. "Now, maybe you'll have time to meet us for lunch."

I didn't look at her.

I didn't look at anyone.

I smiled and sipped my wine, and when an appropriate amount of time had passed, I excused myself to the bathroom. On the way there, in the hallway, I saw Emery standing in the doorway of the mancave. He was staring at me, reading my expression, waiting for me to give him some kind of reaction.

When I didn't, he mouthed, *Are you okay?*

He needed me to be okay tonight, to have his wife with him while he unplugged with his friends and celebrated the Boston project. He needed to have a few drinks and laugh about his buzz on the way home and make love to me the second we got in our bedroom.

For that reason, I mouthed back, *Yes, I'm fine.*

FIVE
JESSE
AFTER

I STOOD in front of the brewing station in my kitchen, holding a cup underneath the spout, and watched it fill with espresso. Using a long spoon, I added some frothed milk and sprinkled some cinnamon and freshly ground nutmeg over the top. This was Emery's favorite way to drink coffee. Because of the time I usually went to work, I would leave his cup on his nightstand, so he would wake up to the aroma.

I no longer had to do that.

I carried both of our drinks into his office where he sat at his large mahogany desk, studying a set of blueprints. I placed his coffee off to the side and moved behind his chair, wrapping an arm around his neck, pressing my lips to the side of his throat. "I asked Luz to pack up several of your suits and have them sent to Boston. I know you already have some there, but a few more can't hurt, especially with how often you'll be traveling."

Luz was our housekeeper in Vermont.

"I also sent Marion a message, letting her know you'll be

visiting weekly, so she can plan accordingly," I said, now referring to our housekeeper in Boston.

He didn't look up from the design he'd been staring at. "You think of everything."

"That's my job."

I breathed through that thought and filled my nose with his scent. There was a constant rotation of different shampoos and soaps in our shower. No matter what he used or the cologne he added after, Emery always smelled like leaves during a spring rainstorm with a hint of spiciness like the cinnamon and nutmeg I'd shaken onto his coffee.

After several deep inhales, I pulled my mouth away, observing how handsome he looked at his desk. He had on a pair of dark jeans and a plaid button-down with a navy sweater on top. And, even though I couldn't see them, he had on argyle socks and dark brown leather shoes.

I just knew my husband that well.

Emery began to move his chair, swiveling it around to face me. When he stopped in front of me, I stepped between his legs, setting my coffee on his desk so that both of my hands were free. My palms went to his cheeks. I loved the way his whiskers felt on my skin. He kept his beard longer in the winter and trimmed much shorter in the summer. Winter was my favorite, and he had reminded me of one of the reasons after Alicia's party when he rubbed it across my entire body.

From the look on his face, I had a feeling he was thinking about the same thing.

"We have the house all to ourselves today," he said, confirming my suspicion. His hands slowly slid to the back of my thighs. "When was the last time I was able to do this"—he rubbed his nose across my navel, air from his lips bursting through my top—"on a weekday?" He continued to wrap around until his fingers were on my butt. His lips slowly parted, his eyes fiery with seduction. "I'm going to put you on top of those blueprints, and then I'm going to—"

"You have an interview in fifteen minutes." I put a finger on his lips. "But I want you to remember the thought you just had, and when the interview is over"—I leaned in a little closer—"I want you to put me on top of those blueprints and do to me whatever it was that you had planned."

He kissed the back of my finger, and it started to tremble.

"You're turning me on so much; I'm shaking," I said, pulling my hand away at the same time the doorbell rang. "She's early. I like that." I slipped out of his grip and took several steps back. "I'll go get her, and we'll meet you in the dining room."

He nodded, and I walked out of his office, still feeling the tremors as I headed down the rest of the hallway. When I looked through the peephole, I was surprised by the tiny girl I saw on the other side. She appeared even smaller as I opened the door, and her frail frame was shivering inside her large down coat.

She certainly wasn't a client of Cinched.

"Tabitha?"

Her smile showed the result of several years' worth of braces. "Th-that's m-me," she chattered, waving her mitten-covered hand. "It's n-nice to m-meet you, M-Mrs. Black-k, I'm ass-assuming."

"Yes." I moved to the side, giving her more than enough room to get past me. "Please come in out of the cold." Once she stepped in and I shut the door, I shook her small, frozen fingers. "Can I get you something warm to drink?"

"I-I'm okay, th-thank you."

"Then, please follow me."

I led her back the same way I had come and brought her over to the table where Emery was already sitting. In front of him, I'd placed two notebooks, pens, and a printout of Tabitha's résumé. If he wanted me involved with the interviews, we were going to conduct them the way I would at Cinched.

"Tabitha," I began when I reached the dining room, "this is my husband, Emery."

"Mr. Black," she said, moving closer to him, extending her hand the same way she had done to me. "It's an honor to meet you."

Once they shook hands, I pointed to the other side of the table and said, "Please make yourself comfortable, Tabitha."

I joined my husband across from her, and the three of us took a seat.

"I asked my wife to join us," Emery said. "I hope that isn't a problem."

"Not at all," she answered. "I've done my own bit of research on you, Mrs. Black. Your achievements are just as impressive as Mr. Black's."

"Thank you," I replied.

I didn't need to look at her résumé to know what it said. I'd already memorized it—along with the résumés from the four other candidates we were interviewing this week. I'd chosen an eclectic group of women—as young as twenty-four, which was Tabitha's age, to as old as mid-fifties. I wanted a range with various levels of skills.

Emery needed to see what was out there.

"Why don't you tell us about yourself?" I said to her.

"I'm a graduate of the University of Connecticut," she began, giving me the feeling that this was well rehearsed. "My first job out of school was with a family in Burlington where I was a nanny for their children, ages two and four. The parents worked nonstop, as I'm sure the both of you do. So, in their absence, I was responsible for their household, doing everything from cooking to driving to doctor visits. I even went with them on family vacations." Her voice was the sound of innocence. And, even though she was several years older than Viv, they looked the same age.

"Why do you no longer work for the family?" he asked.

Emery's stare was on Tabitha, so mine stayed on him as she answered, "They moved to California. They asked me to join them, but my family is here, and I don't want to live far away from them, so now, I'm job-hunting."

He sighed. Tabitha couldn't hear it, but I had. Then, I saw him set the pen down on the table, which, at some point, he'd picked up as though he were going to take notes. Not anymore. He had nothing to write because he'd stopped listening. She had bored him to death before she even got to the nannying part.

This interview was already over.

SIX
CHARLOTTE

SINCE CHARLOTTE COULDN'T PREDICT ALL the questions that would be asked during her interview, she decided to spend several hours each day researching Emery Black. From the articles she read online, she learned he had attended Northeastern University on a full lacrosse scholarship, graduating with a degree in architectural studies. He was offered a job while he was still in school, and within a few years, he was their lead designer. Ten years ago, he had gone off on his own and really begun to make a name for himself in the New England area. Now, he had buildings all over Boston, Portland, Manchester, and Cape Cod. He even had a few in Manhattan and LA. Emery's designs weren't just in high demand; they were award-winning.

In one of the interviews, Emery had discussed his personal life, telling the reporter he had met Jesse his freshman year of college. They lived in the same dorm, two floors apart. They were married by the time they were twenty-five, and Jesse had opened Cinched a few years prior.

In a different interview, this one focused on Jesse, she had been asked what had prompted the business. Her reply had been that she was trying on gowns and couldn't find any undergarments that had the level of support she was looking for. The company was now estimated to be worth a quarter of a billion dollars.

Charlotte thought it would be difficult to find another husband and wife who were as determined, successful, and talented as the Blacks.

Or as gorgeous.

Emery and Jesse had matching dark hair and blue eyes with sharp features that made their faces stand out. They looked perfect together.

Wondering how far their home was from hers, she typed their address into her phone and watched the line form between her dot and theirs. It was four miles away, approximately sixteen minutes. Her last job was less than a mile, and in the summer, she used to bike to work. She wouldn't be able to do that with the Blacks, and she would be tripling her commute.

It would be worth it.

She got up from her desk and went over to the closet. The clothes she had ordered had been delivered yesterday, and she had washed and ironed them this morning. Now, they hung in front of her.

She grabbed a pair of dark gray pants from the rack and held them in the air. They were skinny jeans–style that would pair well with knee-high boots. She then took a black sweater off the shelf and held it over the pants. She would wear her hair down with no scarf. She didn't want the static. And she wouldn't wear too much makeup, just some mascara, a little blush, and a red lipstick—the most important detail of the entire ensemble.

It was a plan.

But, just as she was about to turn around and head for her kitchen, Charlotte remembered a photo she had seen on one of the Blacks' social media accounts. It was a picture of Emery, Jesse, their two kids, and the dog, and they were all wearing white. Even the dog had a white bandana wrapped around its neck.

Gray and black were too drab. Charlotte needed color.

So, she glanced inside her closet again and grabbed a pair of tomato-red jeans and a white top and hung those on the door, adding the knee-high boots underneath to take in the whole outfit. There was certainly nothing subtle about it. She would stand out the second Emery opened the door.

And that was exactly what she wanted.

SEVEN
JESSE
AFTER

TWO INTERVIEWS YESTERDAY, two earlier today, and the last one was scheduled for this afternoon. Out of all of them, the only candidate Emery had shown any interest in so far was the fifty-five-year-old woman who had come in this morning. He liked the amount of experience she had, but she had been ten minutes late, she couldn't find a pen inside her purse, and her sneeze had reached us all the way over to the other side of the table because she hadn't covered her mouth.

She wasn't a good fit.

We still had one more appointment to go, and with about fifteen minutes until she arrived, I went into the kitchen and filled two glasses with seltzer, splashing in some cranberry and fresh lime juice, and then I set them both on the table. On the other side, I placed a bottle of water.

Then, I went into Emery's office, holding on to the doorframe while I said, "It's almost time for the last interview."

He slowly glanced toward me, his face telling me he was

exhausted with the process. "I don't know if I have one more in me."

I just needed him to hang on a little bit longer.

"You do," I assured him. I turned my body but kept my focus on him. "Meet me at the dining room table in a few minutes. I already got you a drink. You want some almonds?"

He gave me a peek of a smile. That was all I needed, just that tiny bit, and I would immediately stop breathing, my heart feeling as though it were going to burst in my chest.

"Yeah," he said, "I'd love some."

Suddenly, that feeling was quickly turning into something else. My thoughts were everywhere. My breathing was becoming labored. He was staring at my mask while, inside, I was falling the hell apart. I was doing everything possible to hide it from him, but I knew I couldn't for much longer.

"I'll see you out there," I said. I turned, trying not to make it obvious by rushing out, but I still hurried along until I got to the library.

Once I was inside with the door shut, I grabbed one of the shelves with both hands and squeezed the wood with my fingers, my face falling between my extended arms.

I just needed to hold on to something, anything.

My throat was tightening. My ears were ringing. My breath was long gone. Somewhere deep inside of me, a pair of hands were wrapped around my throat, and they were getting tighter and tighter and tighter.

And then …

It was over.

I sucked in a mouthful of air, my skin so slick that my hands slipped off the wood. I turned around, now facing the massive shelves in front of me, and I tried to calm my breathing, stopping the tremors shuddering through me.

The panic attacks had been happening more frequently in the last five months. This one had almost occurred in front of Emery. If he had seen me in the library, he would have had questions.

And those were questions I couldn't answer.

I left that thought behind as I walked to my favorite shelf. Starting all the way to the left, I ran my fingers across the spines of the entire Shakespeare collection my father had given to me. I read the titles, and I tried to slow my heart rate as I got into the headspace where I needed to be. And, right before I reached the last book of the collection, I heard the sound of the doorbell.

It was like an alarm.

I hadn't just heard it. I'd felt it, too. All the way through my body, like the tremors that had shaken me earlier.

Once I made sure the mask was on tight, I made my way to the front of the house and opened the door. I swallowed, blinking hard.

And, just as my eyes connected to hers, I heard, "Hi, I'm Charlotte."

She used one hand to hold the strap of her oversize purse, and the other was sliding through the air toward me.

I took in as much as I could—her long lashes, her grin, her dark red nails. "Hi," I said, clasping hands with her. "I'm Jesse, Emery's wife." I still wasn't breathing right, but I was doing the best I could.

Now that I'd been standing in the doorway for a few seconds, I realized it wasn't as cold as yesterday, but it was still freezing out. I wondered why Charlotte didn't have any gloves on. Her hand was warm. Even a little sweaty.

I was sure mine was also, and that was what I continued to think about when I said, "Please come in." Once she was inside, I shut the door and added, "We're going to be chatting in the dining room, so please follow me."

Before I turned around, she shrugged out of her jacket and draped it across her arm, revealing a white top underneath. White wasn't a forgiving color—I stayed away from it—but it looked excellent on her.

Her light-brown hair fell past her shoulders in waves, but my stare went back to the red lipstick every time. It pulled you in, as did her red pants.

I didn't have red in my life.

I left it for women like Charlotte.

I finally put my back to her and led her toward the dining room where I knew Emery would be waiting. As soon as I rounded the corner, I saw him with his hand in the almonds, chewing a mouthful of them. When he heard my shoes on the floor, he faced me, our eyes locked for only a second, and then they moved to Charlotte. She was behind and to the left of me, giving him the perfect view of the both of us.

There was a dip in his gaze, and then he was back on me.

With a smile, I stopped before my husband, turning halfway so that I could see the two of them, and I began the introductions. "Emery, this is Charlotte Scott."

He stood and moved beside me to shake her hand. The hint of the smile was back, just at the corners of his lips. "It's nice to meet you," he said.

"And you as well," she answered.

Her voice wasn't too sweet. It wasn't sassy either. It was this neutral tone that didn't hurt or bore.

"Charlotte, why don't you take a seat and tell my wife and me a little about yourself?" Emery said.

I followed him to my usual chair where I could focus on the woman across from me.

Her résumé said she was thirty-two, from Florida, and a graduate of the University of Vermont. Her first job out of college was as an AP English teacher at the local high school. The rest of her employment history, knowledge, and skill level was higher than what Emery needed.

Charlotte's stare moved between my eyes and Emery's as she said, "I'm happy to tell you about the software programs I'm familiar with and how talented I am on the computer and how efficient I can be with time and how my memory is my most valuable asset, but I would imagine every candidate you bring in here is just as astute as me." Her face was kind with a smile that was already in her eyes. Freckles sat at the tops of her cheeks. Her naturally pouty lips gave her even more expression.

I looked at Emery, and his attention was on Charlotte.

"Keep talking," he said to her.

"I don't need to bore you with my work history either since it's detailed on my résumé."

The lines in Emery's forehead deepened. So did the ones beside his eyes and in his cheeks.

"Who I'd like to tell you about is me, the person off the page, the one sitting across from you right now. Because it's this woman"—she pointed to herself—"who's going to be coming into your home every day."

Emery sat a little straighter, his hand reaching under the

table until it landed on my thigh. That was where he left it when he said, "Go on."

He found Charlotte attractive. That had been obvious from the moment I walked her into the dining room. He wasn't obnoxious about it, nor was he inappropriate. No one would ever even notice. I just knew him so well that I could tell.

I understood why. Charlotte was beautiful.

She was also thirty-two, at an age where life had already kicked in. Where she had learned from her experiences and lost battles she'd desperately wanted to win. She had reached the point where she knew who she was beneath her makeup and skin.

And that was the kind of woman Emery needed on his team.

When Charlotte had said her skills were the same as the other candidates, she was wrong. She had something none of them had, and that was the ability to get my husband to listen.

With Emery's hand still in my lap, I wrapped my fingers over his, and while I stared at his profile, a thought was so clear in my head.

Charlotte will be the perfect assistant for him.

EIGHT
JESSE
BEFORE

"I CAN'T DO THIS ANYMORE."

Those were five words I'd expected to hear from my mother at some point. I was just surprised it had taken her this long to say them. She wasn't a superhero. There was no right way to handle what we were faced with. We were doing the best we could. But there was grief all over our faces. Tiredness. Fear. We were battling to stay positive when all we felt was hopelessness.

She wasn't giving up. She was speaking from a place of honesty.

My father was going to die, and there wasn't a thing any of us could do about it. Neither could any doctor in the state of Vermont. Or the world. I could say that. I'd scanned every medical database that existed and reached out to the doctors who had any experience with my father's disease. In my correspondence, I begged them to enroll my dad in their focus studies, try unapproved medications, Eastern treatments. I even offered to pay cash. All of the responses I'd received said the same thing—we'd exhausted every avenue, and there was nothing left to try.

The current battle was an infection the doctors had been treating for the last two weeks, and there still wasn't a discharge date in sight. The problem was, every time Dad came to the hospital, he would end up staying longer, making the transition back home even harder. Then, he would become sleepier, more agitated. Pain would start from a new spot.

The back and forth was so difficult on him.

It was equally as taxing on my mom. She stayed late every night and returned first thing in the morning. She barely slept and hardly ate. The aids I employed around the clock were to provide the same level of care to my mom as they did for my dad. Sometimes, she accepted the help, but most of the time, she didn't.

Day after day, we asked why.

And we asked when.

And we hurt. Oh God, did we hurt.

"I know, Mom," I finally said in the softest voice. Dad was sleeping, but I would hate to wake him, especially with what I had said.

"I can't ..." Her lips were trembling while she stared at my father.

It was too stuffy in here. She needed air. I grabbed her jacket and told her to follow me, bringing her outside the hospital to one of the benches by the front of the building. When we sat, two feet of space separated us. I moved closer, putting my arm around her shoulders, resting my head against hers.

"I'm drowning, Jesse."

We both were. I didn't come here as long as she did every

day, but I came after work and stayed at least an hour. I made the decisions she couldn't. I oversaw his care even though it looked like she was the one doing it.

"He doesn't want this," she added. "He doesn't want to live this way."

I knew that, too.

But I wanted to keep him alive as long as I could. Losing my father was going to break me. It wouldn't be something I'd ever recover from. And, even though this was the most selfish thing I could ever want, I didn't care.

I needed my father.

"We just have to stay strong," I told her. "For Dad."

"How?" She no longer had to whisper but still did.

Her skin was as white as the snow on the ground. Her bottom lip hadn't stopped quivering. I knew it had nothing to do with the temperature outside. The emotions ravaging her body were preventing her from feeling anything.

"I just want him to look me in the face and tell me it's going to be all right." She gazed at me now, the pain in her eyes causing my stomach to churn. "He'll never be able to do that again, goddamn it. But it's what I need—for me."

I tightened my grip around her. "That's what you have me for, Mom."

"I know, baby." She wrapped her fingers around mine, and I stared back, trying to take some of her pain so that she didn't have to bear it all. "But I want it to be him, Jesse," she cried. "I want it to be my husband."

NINE
CHARLOTTE

CHARLOTTE WAS in the middle of a wine store when she felt her phone vibrate in her back pocket. Thinking it was one of her friends, she stopped in the pinot noir aisle to take out her cell and look at the screen. It wasn't a text like she'd thought. It was an e-mail with the subject, *Job Offer: Executive Assistant for Emery Black.*

She opened it and read the first few sentences. She could tell Jesse had helped Emery write the e-mail. It was formal but with the warmness of a woman. The e-mail congratulated Charlotte on the job offer and explained the two documents attached—one a contract and the other a nondisclosure agreement. If accepting the job, both had to be signed, notarized, and returned immediately. Emery was requesting a Monday start date, which was four days from now, and he wanted a decision in twelve hours.

Charlotte heard someone pass by her in the aisle, their cart getting extremely close to hers. But she never looked up. She was too focused on her phone, pressing the attachment and waiting for it to download. The contract was several pages long, and she began to read each one. It outlined many of her responsibilities, duties they had discussed during the interview. It also detailed an extremely generous salary, three weeks of vacation, and a hefty benefits package she had not expected.

The offer was double than what she had made at her last job.

She opened the nondisclosure agreement and was satisfied with all the verbiage. Working in the home of two extremely successful entrepreneurs, she'd expected there'd be legal documents she would have to sign, and she had no problem doing so.

Once she got home from the wine store, she would read both attachments in detail, get them notarized, and return them to Emery before the end of the day. By the time she got back home, her three girlfriends would just be arriving. It was Thursday, which was girls' night. Charlotte and her friends took turns hosting, and it was Charlotte's turn. This morning, she had picked up several different kinds of cheeses and olives and nuts and fruits. The only thing left to buy was the wine.

The timing of Emery's offer couldn't have been more perfect since, tonight, she would really be able to celebrate.

She had taken a huge risk during that interview, and she was relieved it had paid off.

Charlotte was smiling so hard in the pinot noir aisle; her cheeks began to hurt. She took a deep breath, tucked her phone back in her pocket, and looked at the rows of bottles. Normally, she would have chosen ones in the fifteen-dollar range. She had to buy eight bottles, and that added up quickly. But, with the salary Charlotte had just been offered, she decided to splurge, choosing a few that were double her typical budget. On her way to the register, she grabbed a bottle of champagne, thinking she would kick off girls' night with a toast.

As Charlotte paid for all the items, she decided she would take tonight to unwind, shut off her brain, and celebrate. Because, come Monday morning, everything was going to change. Working for Emery would be an adjustment, and it would challenge her in ways she hadn't been before.

She was ready for it.

TEN
JESSE
AFTER

I STOOD, unnoticed, in the doorway of Emery's office, watching him while he worked. Unless it was a weekend, I rarely had an opportunity to do this. There had only been a handful of mornings before this one when I leaned into the molding and stared at him.

He was worried; I had seen that on his face from the moment he told me he'd been awarded the project. He didn't want to spend too much time in Boston, but he didn't want to spend too little either. This job was paying him millions. It was a lot to process and even more to manage.

While he was away, I would get alone time with my kids, something I'd never had before. And, when he was home, we would be together as a family.

I saw no problem with the new arrangement.

Emery took a pen out of the drawer and wrote something on a pad. His stare moved between the computer and the paper. Each letter was uppercase, all close in height and width, his handwriting like a font. I could see it as clearly as the picture of our children that was framed and facing me on his desk. There was another one of just the two of us in Scotland. The third photo was of our dog, Birdie, our other baby who slept at the foot of our bed every night.

Anyone looking into this house would see a couple, who had been together since they were eighteen years old, with two beautiful children. They would notice I gazed at my husband, not the camera, whenever our picture was taken. We had a dog from a champion line of Labradors, two businesses, two homes, and more money than we could spend in a lifetime.

On the outside, we were envied.

Perfect.

Untouchable.

But, inside our circle of four, there was a weakness.

Me.

Emery slowly turned his head, and our eyes caught. I exhaled, feeling the tightness stay in my throat, even after the air was out of my lungs.

"Why are you so far away?" he asked.

I felt his words in the pit of my stomach. It was a slow burn that moved to the lowest spot in my navel and went as high as my breasts. "I was admiring you."

"Come do it from my lap."

I moved across the room, and when I was within reach, he took my hand and led me around to the front of him.

He kissed me the second I was seated, his arms wrapping around my waist. "What have you been doing?"

I ran my hand across his cheek, feeling the roughness of his whiskers. "I sent the offer to Charlotte, like you'd asked me to. I just came downstairs to get something to eat, and I figured I'd stop by your office to see if you wanted anything."

His nose grazed my cheek. "I like having you home."

"I know."

"I didn't realize how much I'd missed you."

Before I could react, he put both of his hands on my face and pulled me toward his mouth. The second I felt his tongue, his grip tightened, and he said, "Are the kids home?"

He wouldn't know. I was the one who managed their schedules, who made sure Tommy got to where he needed to be even if I wasn't the one taking him. With Viv having her license and own car, I parented her completely different, but I still knew where she was at all times.

"No, honey. They're not home."

"I was hoping you would say that."

He gave me a quick kiss. Then, we were both on our feet, and he was unzipping the back of my fitted skirt. I gasped as the material fell to my ankles. I felt so bare in the lace panties and blouse. I wasn't stable, not with his eyes on me.

"Breathtaking." His compliment wasn't much louder than a whisper, but he might as well have shouted it. That was how noisy it sounded, how consuming it felt when his words entered my ears.

Standing before him like this made me vulnerable. It made the mask want to drop as quickly as my skirt. It made me worry that, if he just looked deep enough, he would see what was really hiding inside me. While his stare roamed my face, I deflected, changing my thoughts, putting my concentration on something much safer than the direction it was headed in now.

And, when I finally opened my mouth, "I need you," came out of it.

I'd never spoken truer words.

"*Mmm*," I heard as he guided me to the edge of his desk.

Once I sat on the thick wood and spread my legs, he began kissing me, and his pants fell to the floor. His tongue filled my mouth at the same time he entered me. His skin slapped against mine, our sounds matching. Heat poured between us as we climbed toward that spot, grinding, gnawing, panting our way there.

Nothing happened slow or gradual on Emery's desk. Our movements were rough, animalistic. Each time his mouth pulled away, our eyes would lock, and the passion between us would smolder again.

And, when Emery reared back his hips, I was lost—in his movements, in the way he loved me, in his ability to make me forget everything, except for the tingling and euphoria happening between my legs.

I wanted to hold on to that for as long as I could. But, within a few strokes, I was shuddering, digging my nails into his shoulders, feeling the burst of sensations spread through me.

Seconds later, while he held my cheeks and pressed his lips against mine, I felt my husband come.

"Charlotte accepted your offer," I said from the doorway of Emery's office several hours after we had sex on top of his desk.

Since he had been designing all day, I knew he hadn't seen her e-mail come in.

He quickly looked across his shoulder. "She already returned the paperwork?"

I nodded, laughing. "You realize I'm acting as your

assistant right now, don't you?" Instead of letting him respond, I said, "Yes, I have everything signed and notarized."

"She didn't try to negotiate?"

"No." I felt my brows rise as I read his expression. "You're disappointed?"

"I wouldn't have settled for the first offer, and neither would you."

We had discussed her salary history during the interview, so he knew we had offered double what she was making at her previous job.

"This is more than she's ever earned," I reminded him.

"She could have gotten another ten percent."

I smiled. "Maybe she'll ask for it after three months. There's nothing in the contract that stops her from doing that."

He was tapping his foot on the floor, his gaze growing more intense every time his toe touched down. "I've been thinking a lot about having Charlotte in our home."

My back went straight, my arm wrapping around my waist. "And?"

"I think she's going to be a good fit."

He was so confident in his answer, and that got a smile out of me.

I'd done so well when I chose her.

ELEVEN
JESSE
BEFORE

I LOOKED at the time on my dashboard, and it showed it was just a little past one in the afternoon. I had been in my car for over two hours. I couldn't recall a single one of those minutes. Not getting in the driver's seat, starting the engine, or pulling out of the parking lot of my father's doctor's office.

But I knew I had done all of those things because, two hours ago, I had been there.

And, now, I was ...

I read the signs on the buildings around me, looking at the people walking past my car. It appeared here was Saint Michael's College—a campus I'd never been to even though it wasn't far from my house. I was parked in a lot with three large brick buildings in front of me. The sign on the middle one said it was a library.

I didn't know what made me remove my seat belt and climb out, but I continued across the pavement, stepping over leaves and rocks and a small puddle from this morning's rainstorm. My fingers were suddenly gripping the cold metal handle, and I was pulling the door open.

"Can I help you?" I heard someone say as I walked inside.

My hand went in the air, fingers waving. I wasn't sure what kind of response that was or how they'd take it, but it was all I had right now. Once my arm dropped, I found myself moving deeper into the room. With each step, the belt from my trench coat squeezed my navel even harder, making it more difficult to breathe. I wasn't sure why I had tied it so tightly. If I had the energy, I would loosen it, but the only thing moving these limbs was adrenaline.

I weaved through several large stacks, and the next time I looked up, I saw some familiar titles across from me. I took one off the shelf and walked with it until I found myself sitting in an oversize leather chair. The book was so old that the paper spine was cracked, and it hit my lap and fell open directly in the middle.

I didn't focus on the people walking past me or the different sounds happening around me.

I didn't think about what had sent me here.

All I did was concentrate on the words.

I wasn't sure if I had been in that chair for an hour or seven. I hadn't looked at a clock from the moment I got to the library. I just knew, at some point, I'd sent Viv a message that told her to pick up Tommy and feed him dinner. Another text had gone to Luz, asking her to make a plate for each of them, taping the heating instructions to the tinfoil.

Once those texts had been sent, I didn't glance up again until I reached the last page. My hands ached as the hardcover rested on them. My mouth was so dry that my lips could barely open.

I needed water.

I needed to get up from this chair.

I needed to change my clothes and wash this morning off of me. I could still taste the vomit in my mouth from when my father's doctor had walked into the room my mother and I had been sitting in and delivered the news to us.

News I'd already known.

News I hadn't wanted him to confirm.

What the hell am I doing here?

I left the book on the table next to me and got on my feet. My legs were stiff and sore. My jacket was still tied too tightly, and my purse hadn't moved from my shoulder, although I didn't even remember bringing it from the car.

I shoved my hands into the pockets of my coat and made my way through the library.

"Have a good evening," I heard on my way out.

It was a different voice this time. It had been a man's voice before; I was sure of it.

I still didn't stop or even look in the speaker's direction. I just rushed for the door, and the darkness outside almost took my breath away. So did the cold when I eventually felt it, the sharpness of it burning my skin. It ached just like the reality I had been faced with today. Like the doctor's expression when he had delivered the results from the final round of tests.

Oh God, why?

The pavement was slick as I hurried across it. Once I reached my car, I threw myself in the driver's seat and started the engine. Before I shifted into reverse, the streetlamp in front of me caught my attention. It was shining through the windshield, the light almost an orange glow.

I didn't know why it happened in that moment. Why it

hadn't occurred earlier or much later that day. But, in my car, under the streetlamp, my mind decided it was time to break down.

A sob came bursting through my lips.

Tears streamed down my cheeks.

It felt like a surge of electricity was moving through my body. Part of me wanted to vomit again. Part of me wanted to tuck my legs against my chest and rock in a ball.

It hurt.

It hurt worse than anything I'd ever felt.

My hand hit the steering wheel and, "Why?" was the only sound that came out. It rolled across my tongue, the syllable holding steady until I ran out of breath.

I knew no one would answer me, but I still screamed it.

Again.

And again.

TWELVE
CHARLOTTE

WHEN CHARLOTTE and her younger sister had been growing up in Florida, Charlotte's mom had had a hard time paying her bills. The small income she'd earned at the gas station wasn't enough to cover rent, utilities, food, the needs of her two kids, and the alcohol she liked to drink when she wasn't at work. Every few months, Charlotte and her family would be evicted from their apartment, requiring the three of them to move again, Charlotte and her sister having to change schools.

She was always the new kid.

But, by being one, it'd taught her how to adapt to unfamiliar situations and to never be afraid to try something new, like an executive assistant position for Emery Black. Despite her knowledge of administrative duties, Charlotte had never actually worked as an assistant before.

She was anxious to start.

And, a few hours after she returned the signed and notarized documents, there was a courier at her door. He handed her a package, and she paused girls' night just long enough to see what was inside. It was a notebook with the word *Everything* written in black Sharpie on the front.

Later that evening, after her friends left, Charlotte climbed into bed and opened the notebook, reading it from front to back. It wasn't quite a manual, more like a CliffsNotes version of everything she would need to know to work in the Blacks' house.

Charlotte's previous jobs had required research and studying, but none of them had ever been quite like this. It would take her weeks to memorize everything on those pages, but she appreciated having them as a reference guide. Still, she wouldn't let herself get overwhelmed. She would embrace Monday with a mindset that it would take time before she was comfortable, but her passion and desire to be there outweighed the painful learning curve the three of them were about to endure.

When her alarm went off the morning of, she shot right out of bed and immediately went into the shower. She dressed in a pair of black pants and a hot-pink top and spent extra time getting her hair just right. Charlotte believed in being early, so eight minutes before nine, she was standing on the front step of the Blacks' house, ringing the doorbell.

She was only there for a few seconds before the door slowly opened. She expected to see Jesse on the other side, welcoming her like she had done the last time Charlotte was here. But it wasn't Jesse.

It was Emery.

Charlotte felt herself take a deep breath, the cold burning her insides, her hands tightening into freezing balls within her mittens. "Emery," Charlotte said. "Good morning."

"Morning." He held the door wider, and Charlotte stepped inside, standing in the foyer while he locked up behind her, eventually turning in her direction. "Now that you have your own code, please feel free to come and go through the side door," he said. "I'd hate to have you out here in the cold, waiting for us to answer the door."

Charlotte had looked at him during the interview but divided her attention equally between the couple. Now that the pressure was off and she had the job, she could really take him in. She hadn't noticed before the rich chestnut color of his beard or the incredibly sexy lines at the sides of his eyes that told her the man liked to smile. She just hadn't seen him do that yet. What she had noticed the other day and again now was that he was even handsomer than in his pictures online. He had a boyish lightness to him yet an extremely mature, distinguished face. He was well dressed on both occasions, and it was obvious he took good care of himself.

"The side door sounds much easier," she replied. "I'll start using it tomorrow."

"Great. Follow me."

Jesse was standing at the counter when Charlotte and Emery walked into the kitchen. Jesse handed him a mug, holding her own in her other hand.

"Happy Monday," she said to Charlotte.

"To you as well," Charlotte replied. She pointed at Emery's cup, remembering what had been written about his coffee preference in the notebook. "A latte with a full tablespoon of whip and a sprinkle of cinnamon and freshly ground nutmeg."

"She's good," Emery replied.

Charlotte blushed and nodded toward Jesse's mug. "What do you prefer? I'm happy to make it for you in the morning."

"That's not necessary," Jesse responded.

"Please," Charlotte said. "I would like to do it."

A few seconds passed before Jesse spoke again, "A regular coffee with a splash of almond milk and a dash of Splenda." When Charlotte smiled at her, Jesse added, "Have you used one of those before?"

Charlotte followed Jesse's finger and wanted to laugh when she realized what she was referring to. This wasn't a regular machine or even a multi-cup brewing system. This was an appliance that had been built into their wall with a touch screen and several levers and an array of spouts.

Charlotte shook her head. "No."

"Don't worry," Jesse said. "We'll go over it today. You'll be an expert by lunchtime; it's easy."

Charlotte had been told through e-mail that, for the first part of the day, she was going to be shadowing Jesse around the home, getting a tour of the property, learning the entire space. Charlotte was relieved this was one of the things they would be covering.

"Do you drink coffee?" Jesse asked her.

"Yes."

"Then, let's make you a cup now."

Charlotte followed Jesse over to the machine. As they stood in front of it, Jesse explained the buttons she was pressing and showed her where the different-sized mugs were located in the cabinets and where to place the cup for the specific kinds of coffee.

"Sweetener is in there," Jesse said, nodding toward a cabinet on the other side once the coffee started to brew.

"Creamer, almond milk, and coconut milk are in the fridge. If there's something else you put in that we don't have, please notify Luz, our housekeeper, and she'll make sure it's stocked for you."

"Creamer will be fine," Charlotte said.

"Same is true for food," Jesse added. "You'll be working long hours, and if you're in my home, I want to feed you. Luz is an excellent chef. Feel free to ask her to prepare anything and to stock whatever you like."

"Thank you," Charlotte said, taking the mug from Jesse's hand.

She went over to the fridge, adding in some creamer that she'd found in the door. Before she shut it, she took a peek inside, seeing that the drawers were filled with fresh vegetables and that the shelves held meats and fishes and dairy and things you wouldn't find in a single woman's fridge. Charlotte loved to cook. She just didn't love to cook for one.

During the interview, Emery had mentioned that there could be occasions where Luz wouldn't be able to stay, and Charlotte would be asked to step in. The same was true for their housekeeper in Boston, and Charlotte would have to make sure everything was taken care of in their home in the city. Now that Charlotte had seen their refrigerator and kitchen, she was looking forward to those evenings. She'd never meal-prepped in a space as beautiful as this one before.

"Let's start by giving you a tour," Jesse said when Charlotte faced her again. Jesse moved next to Emery, and he put his arm around her waist. "In those instances when you might be spending time with our kids, feeding them or taking Tommy somewhere, even staying the night, I want to make sure you're comfortable with that process. In the past, when Luz was unavailable, we relied on friends. We won't be doing that anymore. Emery will now be asking you." Jesse looked at her husband.

"I'll gladly step in whenever you need me to," Charlotte said.

Jesse glanced back at Charlotte and said so warmly, "Wonderful." Then, she turned to Emery and continued, "I'll be seeing you after lunch?"

"Yes."

Charlotte nodded at him just as Jesse said, "Let's get started."

Before Charlotte left the kitchen, she gazed in Emery's direction to see if he needed anything. After all, she was his assistant. What she saw was Emery holding the mug to his lips, his throat moving as he swallowed.

She kept her eyes on him the whole way to the corner and only glanced away because she turned. In all that time, Emery never looked at her once.

That right there made Charlotte smile.

THIRTEEN
JESSE
AFTER

"YOU DID GREAT TODAY," Emery said to Charlotte as she sat on the other side of the kitchen table from us.

Since I had spent the morning with her, Emery wanted me to participate in their end-of-day meeting to discuss how she had done.

"Thank you," she replied. "I really enjoyed myself, and I know I'm going to love working for you." She made sure to speak to the both of us, and that was something I'd picked up on immediately. "Tomorrow morning, I'll let myself in through the side door. I know where I'll find Emery, but where can I bring your coffee to?" she asked me.

During the tour, she had noticed I hadn't shown her my home office. Once I'd moved Cinched out of our apartment, I never brought it back into our house.

Emery rubbed his hand over my shoulder. "Soon, her office will be in the far bedroom in the north wing," he said, stopping to smile, "but for now, I have a feeling you'll find her in the library."

"He's right about the library part." My brows rose. This was the first time I was hearing this news. "My office is going to be where?" I asked Emery.

"We're converting the space for you." He nodded toward Charlotte. "It's the first project I'm having her work on."

"I ordered your furniture this afternoon," Charlotte added, grinning at the both of us. "I put a rush on the order, so they're promising it will be here in a month."

"Emery ..." I heard myself whisper, my eyes solely on my husband. "Thank you."

I knew Charlotte was watching this moment happen between us, something that should probably take place privately. I didn't care. He had known for less than a week that I had pulled back from Cinched, and he had already designed a new space for me and ordered furnishings without my knowledge.

And I knew I would love every inch of it.

This man was so wonderful that it hurt.

Once Charlotte left, I would thank my husband in an entirely different way.

In the meantime, I turned toward Charlotte and said, "I think you did exceptional today. Our time together this morning couldn't have gone better. You seem to have picked up everything with ease." I crossed my legs as Emery's hand slid across my thigh. "Do you have any questions for me?"

"No questions, just a suggestion."

I nodded, urging her on.

"I was thinking I could take Tommy to his art class on Wednesday. That way, I can get familiar with the route to his school and after-school program in case I have to take him in the future."

She hadn't met Tommy or Viv yet. The introduction was going to happen tomorrow. I'd wanted to wait a day just to make sure Charlotte was a good fit before I got the kids involved. Now that I knew how well things were going to go, I believed it was time for her to meet them.

When I swallowed, there was a tightening in the back of my throat. "I think that's a fantastic idea."

"Now, let's talk about Boston," Emery said. He kept his hand on my thigh but scrolled his phone with his other one. "I'd like to go on Thursday, take the first flight out, and get there before breakfast." He looked up at me. "I'll do what I need to at the builder's office, and you can show Charlotte around our place."

Although Emery and I hadn't discussed me joining them, I didn't need to pull up my own calendar to know that I could. There was nothing on it, except for Tommy's activities, which Luz would manage in my absence.

"I think that sounds perfect," I told him.

Charlotte was holding a pen, pressing it against a notebook, prepared to write down whatever we were saying. Every time I had seen her today, she'd been holding both the exact same way.

"Exciting," she exclaimed. "I'll make the arrangements as soon as I get home."

There was so much enthusiasm in her voice that it sounded like she genuinely wanted to go.

I could understand why. Boston was a magical city.

Emery pushed his phone aside, taking a few seconds before he broke the silence. "I look forward to seeing you tomorrow, Charlotte."

She stood from the table. "I'm going to grab my things from

the hall closet, and I'll let myself out through the side door. You both have a great night."

I smiled at her, and as she turned away, I went over to the fridge, grabbing some freshly sliced pineapple and blueberries that Luz had picked up from the farmers market this morning. I poured a little of each into a bowl, took two forks out of the drawer, and brought everything over to the table.

Emery speared a chunk of pineapple with his fork and popped it into his mouth. "I have an idea." He swallowed and followed it with several blueberries. "Why don't we send Charlotte back to Burlington on Friday morning and the two of us can stay in Boston an extra night?" He took in another bite. "I need some time alone with you."

"So, Charlotte—"

"Will pick up Tommy from school to give Luz a break, and she'll make sure he has what he needs before she goes home for the night. Luz will stay with the kids, and we'll fly back the next afternoon after we have brunch on Newbury Street."

I certainly couldn't turn down what he was offering. A night with him in my favorite city, one where it'd all begun for us, sounded like absolute heaven. And the fact that he had thought of it on his own made it even sweeter.

"You'd better let Charlotte know about your change of plans before she gets home and books the tickets," I said.

Emery immediately lifted his phone off the table, and I watched his thumbs press the screen as he typed out a text to her.

When he set his phone back down, I said, "How do you think today really went?"

He ran his hand across the top of his head, messing up the hairs but going over them again to fix. "She seemed to understand everything I'd explained to her, and what I tested her on, she passed."

I laughed. "You tested her?"

"Absolutely." His face was so serious. "How else will I know if she's paying attention?"

I was still laughing when I said, "She's not a child, Emery."

I had to make sure he was aware of that. The last thing I needed was for him to look at her the same way he viewed our daughter and treat her as though she were seventeen, too.

"I know," he replied, tightening his grip on my leg. "I just hate when I have to say things twice."

Good listening skills was one of the top things I'd looked for, and I'd tested each candidate during their interview. Charlotte was the only one who'd passed.

"Have you had to repeat yourself so far with her?" I asked.

"No." He paused. "I'm impressed."

I couldn't have been happier with his response.

I picked up a blueberry and held it against my lips. Just as I was about to bite down on it, Emery's phone beeped.

"It's a text from Charlotte," he said, staring at the screen. "She purchased the airline tickets and forwarded me the confirmation."

I was sure Emery hadn't gotten to his flying preferences during their short time together today; however, all of that information was included in the notebook I had given her. I just hoped she had looked at it first because Emery was a fussy traveler.

I watched him open his e-mail, a smile slowly creeping over his face.

"She got everything right. And ... Jesus Christ."

"What?"

"She booked her hotel, the one that's a few blocks away from our place, and she sent Luz an e-mail, letting her know we'd changed our schedule, so Luz could make herself available for the kids."

She was proving herself.

And Emery was pleased.

I placed my hand on my husband's and gazed into his eyes, my heart starting to speed up, pounding on the inside of my chest. My other hand clenched in a fist, and I pressed it against my stomach. "Sounds like I found you exactly what you needed."

"Baby"—the look he had on told me I could have anything I wanted, and that was when I knew how well I had really done—"you did."

"Mom!" Viv shouted from the front door.

The sound of her voice was no different when she woke up in the morning. She was loud, always making her presence known. I wouldn't have her any other way.

"In the kitchen, baby." I made sure my hands were tightly inside the mitts when I reached into the oven and took out the roasted potatoes and vegetables and the four pounds of haddock Luz had baked.

"Where is everyone?" Viv asked as she came over to the island.

The curls she had put in her hair this morning were gone, and so was most of her makeup. There was worry on her face instead. I had a feeling it was due to the test she had coming up on Friday, and she was thinking about the date she had gone on last weekend. The guy was new to her school, a transfer who had come in for just his senior year. She liked him.

"Tommy is in his room, doing homework, and Daddy is in his office."

"Ugh."

I stopped placing the asparagus on the tray. "What's wrong?"

"I was hoping Tommy would be at art class, so it wouldn't look so bad that I have to bail on dinner."

I placed an onion sliver in my mouth and set the spatula on the baking sheet, so it wouldn't shake in my hand. "Why are you too busy for dinner?"

"I have a paper due tomorrow, and I need every second to finish it."

"Nice try, missy. You're coming to dinner, and I don't want to hear another word about it."

"Mom ..."

I gripped the edge of the counter. "You know the rules. We don't miss family dinner. There are no exceptions."

"But—"

The look on my face told her I wasn't budging, nor was I going to listen to any negotiating. "Go tell your brother and father dinner is ready and get your butt to that table when you're done."

She turned hastily, full of attitude, and headed toward the hallway.

Before she was out of my sight, I shouted, "Viv," across the kitchen. When she faced me, I mouthed, *I love you.*

I glanced down before I saw if she mouthed it back, and I continued to plate the veggies. Once those were on the table, I put a serving of fish on everyone's plate. Drinks were already poured, bread was in a basket, and butter and condiments were there, too.

"It looks delicious," Emery said as he stepped in behind me. He pressed his lips against the side of my neck, his hands gripping my waist.

"Really, guys," our son moaned.

I laughed into Emery's mouth as I was now facing him and moved to my chair. The rest of my family did the same, Viv coming in last. Once she sat, I passed the bread and vegetables, making sure everyone had what they needed before I picked up my fork. As I held it in my hand, I didn't look down at my plate. I stared at the faces that were around this table, and I tried to live in this second for as long as I could.

The room was filled with Viv's gorgeous laughter and Tommy's beautiful smile.

I was filled by the way my husband was looking at me. It was a smolder I could feel in my entire body.

"I'm glad you made me stay, Mom," Viv said, causing that fire to go out.

My eyes flitted across the table. It took a while to get there, but when they finally locked with my daughter's, I felt a love that was indescribable. Something I hadn't known existed until the moment I heard her first cry.

"It wouldn't be the same without you, baby," I replied.

I looked back in Emery's direction. The intensity from a few seconds ago was gone, and in its place was so much warmth. He was happy. Things had gone better than he planned. Charlotte was going to give my husband all the help he needed, and now, I was going to focus on my kids.

FOURTEEN
JESSE
BEFORE

FOUR DAYS HAD PASSED since I ended up at the library at Saint Michael's College. Time wasn't just moving; it was slipping away. And, following the meeting with my father's doctor, I just hadn't been able to get a grasp on everything that was happening. Hours became blurry. I was missing meetings and reports and forgetting to answer questions.

I didn't care.

I was in this robotic pattern—up long before the sun rose, awake and dazed when I should have been sleeping.

I didn't know how to fix this feeling. How to go back to the way things had been before. How to try to find some normal again. I just knew, after several days of battling these emotions, I couldn't see another e-mail come in, adding to the thousands that were already there. I couldn't send another call to my voice mail, knowing I probably wouldn't phone them back.

I had to get out of here.

I had to make this feeling go away.

I left my desk and slid into the driver's seat of my car.

When I pulled onto the street, I didn't head in the direction of home. Home didn't make me feel any better. I was as unsettled there as I was at work.

So, I drove.

The next thing I knew, I was pulling into the parking lot of Saint Michael's College, in a spot where I could see all three buildings with the library in the middle.

"Good afternoon," I heard someone say as I walked through the door.

There had been two voices the last time I was here—a man when I arrived and a woman when I left. Although I wasn't confident, I had a feeling they would sound familiar if I heard them again.

One thing I knew for sure was the woman who had just greeted me wasn't either of them.

"Hi," I replied to her, and then I made my way toward the back of the library.

I didn't have a destination. I couldn't recall the layout or the area where I had wandered before or the chair I had sat in. There was just something pulling me deeper into the stacks. Maybe it was the smell of books that I loved so much. Maybe I just wanted to be farther away from the door. Maybe it was a feeling that was driving me.

I didn't know.

But I kept on walking past the shelves, my eyes falling onto titles, the tips of my fingers dragging across spines the same way they did at home. I didn't stop until a book caught my attention, and I held the small, extremely old hardcover against my palm.

I hadn't read this one. I'd been meaning to for years. It was part of my father's collection, and he'd been recommending it for a while.

I used to spend so much time in my parents' library when my father was well. Now, the only time he left his bedroom was to go to the hospital, which meant, when I was at their house, I stayed at his bedside.

So many books had gone unread since he became sick. My time went to him. And, when I climbed in bed at night, previously reading until my eyes closed, the desire to pick up a book was gone.

Maybe, one day, I would read again.

As I really started to focus on that thought, I heard, "It's right over here," from what sounded like a woman several aisles behind me. Her voice was so familiar. "It's no problem at all," she added. The closer she got, the more I recognized her. "It should be ... yes, here it is." She stood at the mouth of the aisle, looking at a book on one of the shelves. "Happy reading," she said, giving it to the woman who stood beside her.

She had a young voice.

When she started to walk away, I said, "Excuse me," causing her to glance in my direction.

I waved her over, and she made her way down my aisle.

"Can I help you with something?" she asked.

Her name tag said, *Bay*. It was unique, and I wondered what the story was behind it. Every name had a story. I sensed hers was more interesting than inheriting her mother's maiden name, which was mine.

"This is going to sound silly," I began. "But I was here the other night and ..." I paused, trying to think of the right way to word this.

"And I told you to have a good evening when you were walking out."

"Yes." I backed up until I felt the shelf press into my shoulders and another one at my waist. "That was me. I ..." I lost my train of thought, unsure of where I was even going with this.

Or why I had come here.

Or what I was doing in this aisle right now.

"Is everything all right?" she asked.

I knew I was breathing, but I couldn't feel myself suck in any air. I couldn't feel anything. It was as though I was standing here without my mask, and this girl was seeing me.

Really seeing me.

"Yes," I answered. "I think I'm okay."

"No ..." She was smiling, shaking her head. "I don't mean, if you're okay right now. I mean, the other night, when you were leaving the library. Whatever was bothering you, I hope it all worked out." She was standing close, the side of her body leaning into the same shelves as me.

"How did you know something was wrong?" The words had come right out, but I didn't regret them.

"It was the expression on your face." Her stare shifted from my right eye to my left. "It's hard to explain, but it's one of those looks when you see it; it really hits you."

I understood.

More than she knew.

It was probably the same one my mother had worn when my father's doctor delivered the news.

The thought of that made me tighten.

Everywhere.

There was nothing left to say besides, "I'm sorry." Now that

I remembered, it was the reason I had come here anyway. "And I want to apologize to the man who greeted me when I came into the library. At least, I think it was a man; I can't be sure."

"His name is Gregory." Her hand went to my shoulder. "What's your name?"

"Jesse."

"Jesse, I'm Bay."

I smiled. "I know. I saw your name tag."

"You don't owe me an apology." She squeezed a little tighter. "You did nothing wrong that night."

I sighed. "That's the reason I came here—because I wasn't sure what had happened. Most of that day is just white fog, so I wanted to speak to you and Gregory and make sure I didn't do anything to embarrass myself."

Is that even true?

Is that the real reason I'm here?

I had no idea anymore.

"You were fine; trust me." Her hand fell from my shoulder. "It was nice to meet you, Jesse," she said, and then she walked away.

I said it back to her.

After a few steps, she turned toward me and added, "That's a good one." She was nodding at my hand, which was still holding the small hardcover.

"You've read it?"

"Yes, and it's one of my favorites."

"About that night"—I took a breath—"I just want you to know I'm okay."

I had no idea why I'd told her that. I didn't know this girl. What she thought meant absolutely nothing to me. But, for some reason, I'd had to say those words, and for the same reason, she'd needed to hear them.

"You don't look all right."

A laugh burst through my lips. Nothing she had said was funny. I was just so taken aback by her honesty.

It was as though she had the formula to unstick my mask. Or maybe, when she gazed at me, she didn't see one at all.

"I thought I was doing an excellent job at hiding it."

"Don't we all think that?" she said. "It takes a hider to know one."

Something wedged into my throat, pushing all of my feelings to the surface, and words started to come out. "It's ... my dad ..." I looked down. I didn't want her eyes on me. I didn't want to see her pity. It would make me cry, and I didn't want to do that again today. "He's not well. It's something we've been dealing with as a family for a very long time. And the other day ... the doctor shared the latest results and ..." I shook my head. It was all I could do. "It's not good."

She walked back over, her hands now on my shoulders, sandwiching me between her palms. It was oddly comforting.

"I would ask if you needed any information on his disease, but if you've been dealing with it for a long time, then you're well versed."

"I'm fluent."

"Is there anything we can do here to help?"

"I came here when I needed to escape. That's more than enough."

She nodded, squeezing both sides of me before her hands dropped, and she stepped away. "Don't rush out. Stay and read if you have the time. Maybe give that book you're holding a shot." She glanced at her watch. "We're open for another eight-ish hours. It's your choice."

She said nothing more and walked away.

But, that afternoon, it was as though she had written me a prescription. And, for some reason, I chose to take it.

I carried the book to the nearest chair, and I began to read. Within a few pages, I remembered what I'd loved about getting lost in a story, how it would hold me captive, fully immersing me with nothing but plot and characters filling my head.

That afternoon, I was reminded of why I needed to make more time for reading.

It sounded so simple, but that day, Bay had changed my life.

FIFTEEN
CHARLOTTE

AFTER DELIVERING Jesse's coffee to her in the library, Charlotte brought Emery's latte into his office and set it on a coaster on the side of his desk. There were two chairs she could sit in. Charlotte chose the one farthest from his computer screen but the one that had the best angle of it. She placed her notebook on her lap, pen already in her hand.

"I want to talk about Boston," he started.

"Okay."

"When I'm there, I need to fully be there. That means, I need to know my other projects will get the amount of attention they require. And I need to know Jesse and my kids will be all right while I'm gone." Emery paused, and Charlotte got the impression he was far from done. "We lost Jesse's father two months ago. It was a horrible death, and we've all been extremely shaken up about it. As for my wife, she's not even close to recovering." Emery scratched an invisible crumb off his desk. "She recently stepped back from her company, and she's going to be spending a lot of time at home with the kids."

"I'm so sorry for all of you."

"Charlotte ..." He paused as though he needed to gather his thoughts. "I need to know she's going to be okay while I'm gone. I realize, a majority of the time I'm in Boston, you'll be there with me, so I don't know how you're going to accomplish this, but I need you to."

"I'll take care of it. You have my word."

He took a drink of his coffee, and when he pulled his mouth away, he looked down at the whip. "You added extra cinnamon and nutmeg."

"Jesse's notes didn't specify how much; it just said a sprinkle, so I guessed."

Charlotte couldn't tell if he liked what she had made or not, but he went in for another sip. And then one more before he set the mug down.

"Do you have any restrictions when it comes to traveling?"

She shook her head. She was extremely single, not even the parent to a pet. "None. I'm available to go to Boston—or anywhere else—whenever you need me to."

"I'm glad that's the case." He reached behind him and took one of the atlases off the shelf, opening it on top of his desk. With a mechanical pencil, he pointed to a spot toward the center of the map. "This is the location of the project we're going to be working on." He made a circle on the paper. "It will be sixty-two stories tall with three levels of commercial space, four for parking, and the rest will be residential. It's the most efficient and innovative of all my designs."

Charlotte was so impressed with the way he'd spoken about the building; her skin was covered in goose bumps. This wasn't just a job for Emery. This was a passion and the reason he was award-winning and so in demand. She couldn't believe how inspiring it was to see someone at this point in their career.

"What does the building look like?" she asked.

According to her research, the builder for 3 Stuart Street hadn't yet revealed who they'd hired as an architect, and they hadn't shown any mock-ups of the design.

"I can show you if you'd like."

Charlotte nodded. "I would love that."

Emery placed one hand on his keyboard and the other on his mouse, and after several clicks, there was a three-dimensional diagram on his large computer screen, revealing every detail of the massive high-rise.

She leaned her body into the desk, so she could get in even closer, and she stared in awe as the image shifted, showing her all the different views of his masterpiece. "It's brilliant," she said.

"It's going to change Boston's skyline." He laughed. "No pressure or anything."

This was the first time Emery had really loosened up in her presence, and Charlotte was relieved to finally see it. She had known it would take time. This was only her second day, so she was glad it had happened this soon. The lightness in his expression showed the beauty in his eyes. They were a medium blue—a mix between a mid-morning sky and the waters of the Caribbean. Charlotte thought they were piercing.

"You're going to do great," she said. "Besides, you're heroic now; people are going to be admiring you even more."

He waved his hand in the air, like he was dismissing what she'd said. But Charlotte's declaration was the truth. Emery was going to be part of Boston's history, which would make him even more in demand.

"I feel the need to warn you that it's not going to be an easy project," he said. "Boston always adds its own set of complications—sometimes, starting in the ground; other times, because of the weather."

"I'll make things as easy as possible for you then."

Emery took his hand off the mouse and surrounded the handle of his mug, lifting it to his lips again. He watched Charlotte as he swallowed, eventually putting the cup back down. "There's a lot to learn in order for you to do that."

She was already near the end of her chair, but she moved to the very edge of it and said, "Teach me. I'm ready."

That was the second time Charlotte saw Emery smile that morning.

But it was the first time he smiled at something she'd said.

SIXTEEN
JESSE
AFTER

"I UNDERSTAND," Emery said into his phone as he held it against his ear. "I'll edit it the minute I get to my computer."

My husband had been on his cell since the moment we landed in Boston almost forty minutes ago. Now, we were in the back of the SUV Charlotte had ordered for us, and I could tell his conversation wasn't going the way he wanted it to.

"I'll make it work," Emery said. "I'll see you soon." He hung up but kept his cell in his hand, his fingers tapping the screen. He was aggravated; anyone could tell that by the way he was typing. "Charlotte," he called out.

She turned around from the passenger seat with a notebook and pen in her hand.

"Last night, I forwarded you information on two different private airline companies. Contact the first one, the one based on the East Coast, and set up an account. I'd like us to be able to start flying private by next week."

What made me happy about this decision was that he realized how critical his time was, and he didn't want to spend it in an airport, dealing with delays or cancellations. He wanted to get there and get home to his family. And it made me even happier he had come to this realization on his own.

"I'll take care of it," she replied.

To lighten the mood, I looked at Charlotte and said, "I'm sure Emery showed you the location of the jobsite. But he probably pulled out an atlas and gave you the longitude and the latitude of the property instead of saying it's four blocks from our brownstone and three from where you'll be staying."

She was blushing, which told me that was exactly what he had done. I laughed at the image that had popped into my head. My husband could be so intoxicating yet so nerdy at times.

"Today, you'll be meeting one of Emery's assistant designers."

"Oh, you must be talking about Adam."

I nodded. I didn't know how much Emery had told her, so I continued informing her on their process, "When Emery is in Boston, the two of them typically work in our home. There will be plenty of room for you in there, too. And, if I know my husband, I'm sure one of you has already ordered a third desk."

"It'll be delivered in a few weeks," Emery said, finally glancing up from his phone. "Ricco promised he'd start it today."

The original desk Ricco had made was a gift I'd given to Emery when we first purchased our brownstone. Ricco designed and crafted wooden furniture, and Emery had been admiring his work for a while. When I'd finally gotten the dimensions of the office, I'd called Ricco and had him make a custom piece.

When Adam had joined Emery's team, he'd reached out to

Ricco and had him make an extension. In Emery's space, all the desks had to match, which was why I was positive he had done the same for Charlotte.

"That man is booked years in advance," I said to Emery. "He must really love you."

"I might have promised him some drawings for a house in the Cape he wants to break ground on this fall."

I reached across the seat, pressing my hand against the side of his face. "Now, it makes perfect sense."

The SUV suddenly came to a stop, and I saw we had pulled up to our townhouse.

I looked at Charlotte and said, "I'll give you a quick tour, and then I'll get you over to the hotel."

"Works for me," she replied.

The driver opened my door first. I climbed out and waited for Emery. He grabbed Charlotte's bag—the only luggage we had brought since everything Emery and I needed was already at our home—and the three of us went inside.

Our Boston home was so different than Vermont. Where Burlington was built around the view, the interior all wood and floor-to-ceiling windows so that the mountains were the focal point, Boston was all about the texture. Emery wanted the interior to feel like the city, so he'd made the lines and points extremely sharp and used neutral colors but thrown in pop with high arches and slanted beams and radius edges.

"Wow," Charlotte said from behind me.

I turned around, and so did Emery.

Her face was slightly flushed, her hand over her mouth. "Sorry, it's just"—her head tilted back, and she glanced up at the staircase—"beautiful."

Emery smiled as he listened to her.

It was that look he had on right now that melted me. The one where he got to see firsthand how his designs affected people and the grin that came over his face from the compliment. With Charlotte, it wasn't just her words he got to hear, but he also got to watch her gawk in amazement.

I was thankful I'd gotten to witness it.

When Charlotte finally looked at him, he said, "Thank you," and he moved over to the base of the stairs. "When Adam arrives, send him up."

"No problem," Charlotte answered.

She always responded, showing him she was listening. I was sure he loved that.

"Hey, Charlotte," I said. "Marion, our housekeeper, is around here somewhere. Why don't you ask her to make Emery something to eat? He's usually starving after flights, and he's going to have a long day."

Charlotte smiled. "I'll be happy to."

"This will give you a chance to meet Adam, and then we can do the tour after they leave."

Her lips parted, the original grin returning to her face—the one she had been wearing when I knew she would make the perfect assistant. "I'll go find Marion, and I'll be listening for the doorbell, so I can take care of Adam. When I'm done, I'll come find you."

Once she walked away, I rushed into our master bathroom, locking the door behind me. I didn't even make it a step before the tears began to flow.

I'd promised I wasn't going to cry today.
I'd promised I wasn't going to let it hurt.
Both happened.
And today hurt even more than yesterday.

SEVENTEEN
EMERY

MY WIFE HAD four different laughs.

There was the one that was just a giggle, her way of being kind, letting you know she was paying attention.

And she was.

That woman was always listening.

Then, there was the sound she made when she was entertained. It was a few chuckles, nothing more, with a faint smile.

There were also the times when she actually found something funny. Her giggle would still be on the gentler side, but it would be fulfilling. Her eyes would squint, and there would be a sparkle to them. A glow. She'd turn her head to the side, showing you a glimpse of her nose, the slender slope as she scrunched it. Her already-high cheeks would arch even more. Those stunning lips would spread wider.

If my wife were a design, I wouldn't change a single feature.

She was gorgeous. I'd thought that since the moment I met her. It was even truer now. Not because she had given me two of the most incredible kids. Not because we'd made it through some dark times when we weren't even sure there was another side to reach. Not because, at night, she gave me her body and let me relentlessly ravish it.

Those things had nothing to do with why I thought my wife was even more gorgeous now than when I'd met her our freshman year in college.

That reason was because I saw the woman she'd started off being and the wife and mother she had grown into. Her journey was as beautiful as she was.

She had one more laugh, and it was my favorite.

It was reserved for times when she found something so funny that she lost herself. She would take the deepest breath, and her mouth would open wide; as she laughed, she would look up toward the sky. What came out was the most cheerful, hilarious, addictive sound I'd ever heard.

When she was empty of air, she would take a large breath, recharging her lungs, and the same sound would come out again. Sometimes, it would last up to a minute. She wouldn't be able to stop. You wouldn't want her to. She was that pretty to watch, that mesmerizing.

Jesse drew people in.

It didn't matter where we were; they constantly looked at my wife. But when they had the chance to talk to her was when they got to experience her strongest quality. And that was her ability to really listen, giving a type of attention you never had before. She didn't rush you; she didn't interrupt or cut you off. She just stared into your eyes and heard every word.

It was a quality I'd never seen in anyone else.

Until I met Charlotte.

EIGHTEEN
JESSE
AFTER

"I'LL BE THERE to pick up Tommy from school tomorrow," Charlotte said right before she climbed out of the front seat of the SUV. "I'm looking forward to spending the afternoon with him." She waved at the both of us. "Good night, you two."

"Good night," Emery and I replied in unison.

The driver pulled away from her hotel and was heading toward our home. Emery and I were in the backseat, still recovering from the two-and-a-half-hour-long dinner we'd just had. Since he hadn't left the builder's office until eight, the meal started late. After a few glasses of wine, none of us had seemed to be in a rush. Charlotte was the only one who had to work tomorrow anyway, flying back to Vermont and going straight to our house.

Our plans didn't involve getting up early. We were going to have brunch and spend the day in the city. We would start by looking for a piece of art for my new home office in Burlington. We'd then head downtown and grab a latte in Quincy Market. When we returned to the Back Bay later that afternoon, we'd take a walk down Massachusetts Ave., crossing the Charles River into Cambridge to see the skyline of the city. It was a tradition we did every time we came, even when we brought the kids.

Just on the other side of the river was where Emery had taken me on our first date. We were firm believers that one should never forget where they had come from or what had gotten them there, which was why we always made it a priority to go and visit the spot.

Before I got excited about the plans for tomorrow, I needed to enjoy what was going to happen tonight. Time with just my husband was what I had been looking forward to most about this trip. With Charlotte no longer in the car, I was finally getting what I wanted.

When we got into bed tonight, there wouldn't be a dog at our feet. There wouldn't be kids a wing away.

It would just be Emery and me.

And I could be as loud and as unruly as I wanted.

There were multiple times throughout the night when I'd sensed Emery was thinking the same thing. A slight smile would spread across his lips, and it would cause a tingle in my body. Then, there were the times he'd reached under the table and put his hand on my thigh. It would only stay a few seconds. Just long enough to tease his touch. But, in that time, my husband had made me feel desired and so incredibly sexy.

The slickness between my legs all night was the result of that.

I sighed, watching him gaze out the window, the blocks between the hotel and our townhouse passing by. "Today was good," I told him.

"It was."

He turned toward me, and I immediately saw how unplugged he was.

Emery had been so uptight when he returned from the builder's office. While he was in the shower, I poured him a dirty martini and laid out his clothes. He drank it as he got dressed, and as we drove to the restaurant, I'd heard it kick in. Once alcohol hit Emery's bloodstream, his voice would change.

I rested my hand on his cheek, his beard scratching the inside of it. Sometimes, I would rub it, and other times, I would keep my fingers steady, but it was always his cheek I reached for.

"Charlotte did really well again today." After wiping my face and putting myself back together, I'd found Charlotte and taken her around our home, showing her where everything was, the same way I'd done in Vermont. "I brought her to the jobsite and the hotel, so she's comfortable with both routes."

"There was a lot thrown at her this week."

I chuckled, my hand falling from his face. "I'd say so."

Before my fingers landed in my lap, he caught them and softly kissed the top of my nail. Just as he was moving on to the next finger, my phone began to vibrate inside my purse. When I pulled it out of my bag, I saw it was a text from Viv, a selfie of her and Tommy. They had toothbrushes in their mouths and were making adorable faces in the mirror.

God, they're beautiful.

Emery took out his phone a few seconds later and was looking at the same picture.

"We have the best kids," I said.

"Jesse, it's past eleven thirty, and they're just going to bed now. They have school in the morning. What the hell is Luz doing over there?"

The two things Emery was strict about were academics and bedtime, believing they ran in conjunction.

"I'm sure she was just letting them have a little fun; that's all." I brushed my fingers through the back of his hair.

"If she can't get them to go to sleep at a reasonable hour, then maybe Charlotte should be the one staying with them."

I didn't need to say anything. I could see he'd already made up his mind.

"You know what, that's exactly what's going to happen," he said. "I'll text Charlotte in the morning and let her know the new plan. At some point, we'll need her to stay, so she might as well get comfortable with it now."

I rubbed my hand across his chest and gave him a smile, using both to encourage him to stay calm. The last thing I needed was for him to get really angry. "I'm sure the kids will love having Charlotte there."

His face nuzzled into my neck, and his arm went around my back, using it to pull me closer. I knew I had completely become his focus when he said, "It's a good thing we're almost home."

Each word was a burst of hot air on my tingly skin, and I let out the softest moan just as the SUV came to a stop. Taking Emery's hand, my feet sliding onto the ground, I followed him inside our house. He hung our jackets in the hall closet, and suddenly, I was wrapped in his arms, standing in the middle of the foyer.

And we were dancing.

There wasn't any music; Emery hummed, and that was enough.

My hand was gripped in his and pressed against his chest while my other rested on his shoulder, his on the center of my back. I was shadowing his movements, wrapped in his body, feeling how much he wanted me with each step.

"Gorgeous," he whispered into my cheek.

He was so tender and romantic when I needed him to be. But heat was flowing into his fingers as they lowered, stopping on my ass.

"Emery ..." It was a plea.

He heard it.

Still holding my hand, he brought me to the stairs and led me to our bedroom. Once we were through the door, our clothes began to come off. After the day he'd had, I'd expected there to be an urgency in his movements, a roughness where he thrust inside me the second I hit the bed, my body helping him to work his stress off.

But his mouth was kissing down my navel instead, and he said, "I need to taste you," against my inner thigh.

My hand went into his hair, and I twisted his locks around my fingers, pulling harder, the closer he brought his mouth. He was taunting me, teasing the perimeter, his tongue eventually landing on that deliciously sensitive spot.

He licked until I was clinging to the comforter, my back arching, my heels digging into the bed. Until I was shouting, "Emery," across the bedroom. Until I was bucking against his mouth, getting friction from the point of his tongue.

When I stopped shuddering, he stayed between my legs but moved to his knees, gripping my sides and lifting me to meet him. He hissed when he entered me, a sound I'd fallen in love with the first time I heard it.

"Yes," I breathed, clenching around him.

He brought his face up to mine, his lips barely resting against my mouth. I rocked my hips forward to welcome him in and back to slide him out.

And then in again.

I held him there.

Squeezing.

Emery's fingers were like teeth, biting into my skin. "Jesse ... you feel so fucking good."

Those words started the build inside my body. "Faster," I cried.

He turned me to my side and drove in from behind, his arm crossing my chest, his legs scissoring mine.

"*Ahhh*," I groaned, my husband quickly reminding me how fast that sensation could return.

I was tightening.

He was grunting, moving quicker. Deeper.

And, while we clutched each other, we broke at the same time.

After he pressed his lips against my cheek, keeping them there while we found our breath again ...

After we stilled ...

After he fell asleep and I lay awake, my mind racing with every thought ...

I knew one thing.

I was so lucky to have him.

NINETEEN
CHARLOTTE

CHARLOTTE PULLED up to the front of Tommy's school and waited for the bell to ring. Before she left the Blacks' house, she'd cut up a green apple and filled a small Tupperware container with peanut butter, putting it all into a cooler along with a thermos of water. The notebook, which had information on Viv and Tommy, said nothing about bringing a snack or drink to the pick-up. It was something Charlotte had thought of on her own. Both times she had seen Tommy this week, that was what he had been eating, so she figured the surprise would be well received.

When Charlotte had been in the back of the taxi this morning, on her way to the airport in Boston, she'd gotten a text from Emery, asking if she would stay the night. Charlotte had replied that she would be happy to, but minutes later, she'd begun to worry about the overnight. She'd only seen Tommy and Viv twice before, both instances extremely short. She didn't want her presence to make them feel uncomfortable or seem like she was invading their space.

Charlotte knew a little something about having someone new in your home, spending a lot of time there, having to adjust to it. That'd happened every time her family was evicted. Before she even had her toothbrush unpacked in their new place, her mom would be inviting the neighbors over to drink. Charlotte and her sister learned to tolerate them. But, for as long as they'd lived in their mother's home, they'd felt uncomfortable. She didn't want Viv or Tommy to ever feel that way about her.

She'd only been waiting a few minutes when she saw Tommy exiting the school and heading toward Jesse's car, which she'd been instructed to take. As he got closer, she wondered what she would talk to him about during the drive. Since she only had nieces, she knew the language of girls and how to keep the conversation going. But she had very little experience with boys; therefore, she had no idea what to discuss with him.

"Hi, Tommy," she said as he opened the door.

"Hey, Charlotte." He got in and reached for the seat belt, missing the buckle several times before finally locking it into place.

He was awkward, at the age where he hadn't yet grown into his body. He was still an adorable kid with blue eyes that were as piercing as his dad's and beautiful olive skin like his mom.

"Are you hungry?" Charlotte asked as she put on her blinker.

"Kinda."

Charlotte pointed to the small cooler on the floor of the passenger seat. "Open it."

She pulled into the road as Tommy opened the lid and peeked inside.

"Oh, sweet." He immediately popped a slice into his mouth with a gob of peanut butter.

Charlotte smiled as she saw how pleased he was. "I'm sure your mom told you that I'd be staying with you guys tonight."

He nodded. "She texted me during lunch."

She approached the red light and looked at him. Tommy was on the quieter side. If a conversation was going to happen, Charlotte would have to initiate it.

"Luz didn't have time to cook anything for dinner," she said. "Is there something you're in the mood for?"

He was balancing his phone on one knee and the snack on the other. And, while he was eating, he was swiping his screen and typing, getting peanut butter all over it. She laughed inwardly as she thought about her nieces and how they did the same thing and that she'd need to wipe down the seat tomorrow.

Tommy shrugged. "I don't know."

Charlotte's nieces were notorious for not being able to decide on what they wanted to eat, so Charlotte had come up with a plan ahead of time just in case he was the same way. "I have an idea," she said, "but you have to do your homework and finish by four."

He glanced up from his phone. "Why?"

Charlotte turned onto the Blacks' street and said, "I have a feeling your sister's home from school. I'm going to wait and tell you both at the same time."

"Oh, come on," he groaned. "Viv always hears things before I do. Let this one time be my chance."

She laughed, remembering the competition she'd had with

her own sister when she was his age. "Nope, I'm not budging."

"Ugh."

"How about this? I'll give you a hint." She grinned at Tommy as she turned to go up their long driveway. "It's something artsy."

"Really? Like—"

"No more clues," she said. "You're going to have to wait just a few more minutes for your sister, but at least you know more than she does, right?"

"True."

Charlotte parked behind the garage and turned off the engine. She walked up to the side door and entered her code. Since Viv's car was in the driveway, Charlotte knew she was home and found her in the kitchen when she entered with Tommy.

"Hey," Charlotte said to her.

Viv was sitting at the island, working on her laptop, with two books open in front of her. She briefly glanced up and said, "Hey, guys."

"Viv, hurry up and finish. Charlotte has something fun planned for us." Tommy sat on the other side of the counter, circling an apple around in the peanut butter.

"You planned something?" Viv asked Charlotte.

Charlotte didn't know how to read her. She wasn't an easygoing seventeen-year-old. She was headstrong and opinionated and complex. Charlotte knew that had a lot to do with her age, but that didn't make her job any easier.

"A friend of mine owns a pottery studio," Charlotte started, "and she invited us to come in tonight and make something."

"No way!" Tommy cheered.

Charlotte knew Tommy would like this since art was his thing. The harder sell would be Viv, but Charlotte had a plan.

"Now that your dad is going to be spending more time in Boston, he needs some things on his desk. I was there yesterday, and it's looking terribly bare."

"You're saying we should make him ... pottery?" Viv asked.

Charlotte still couldn't read her reaction. "I thought we could make him a few geometric-style planters." She took out her phone and tapped the screen, showing them the examples she had saved earlier. "We'll keep them small, and we'll put succulents inside after they're done. They'll fit the vibe of his office, and it will make him think of you guys every time he looks at them."

"Sounds cool," Viv replied. "I'm in."

Such a compliant reaction from the Blacks' daughter wasn't what Charlotte had expected, but she was pleased.

"Since we'll be out past your normal dinnertime, how about we grab some pizza on the way home?" Charlotte then suggested.

"Pizza is a definite must," Tommy responded.

Viv didn't have the same excitement on her face. "What if I'm not in the mood for pizza?"

Charlotte walked over to the roll of paper towels, ripped one off, and set it in front of Tommy. "They have a huge menu, Viv. You can order anything you want."

Viv looked at her brother and then back at Charlotte. "I guess I'm good with that."

This felt like such a massive victory that Charlotte wanted to celebrate. But she knew this was only the beginning, and she hadn't even come close to winning over Viv.

Still, this was a hell of a start.

TWENTY
JESSE
BEFORE

"WHAT ARE WE GOING TO DO?" my mother said from the other side of the bed.

It was the bed she shared with my father. There was a half-empty bottle of wine on Dad's nightstand, where I'd placed it before I climbed onto the mattress, and there was a glass in each of our hands. I didn't know if this was the appropriate moment to drink. I didn't care. Both of us needed it.

Oh God, did we need it.

When I had seen the bottle in the kitchen, I'd grabbed it off the shelf, found an opener, and brought it right in here. I hadn't known what it tasted like. I hadn't known if it was red or white.

It hadn't mattered.

After what had felt like hundreds of tests, not a part of my father's body that hadn't been poked or scanned, we'd finally gotten the results today.

Before walking into the doctor's office, we had known

there was a problem. We had known there were possibilities. But we'd had no idea what we were in for.

Now, thirty minutes later, we were in their bed because we didn't know where else to be.

"I don't know, Mom," I finally replied.

Since I was an only child, it had always just been the three of us. We did everything together still. I was as involved with his doctor visits as my mother. So, when the doctor had spoken the diagnosis, we'd heard it together as a family. It passed through all six of our ears. My father's first, as he was the closest to the doctor. Then, my mom and me. Once he finished giving us the news, I grabbed my mom's hand and squeezed it.

I needed to hold on to something.

I knew she did, too.

The second our fingers linked, she was clutching me, using a strength I never knew she had. My skin was screaming as her nails dug into it, but I needed the pain. It had given me something to focus on besides the torture happening in my heart.

"Baby ..." Her voice broke at the last syllable, and I turned toward her.

My mother wasn't a woman who moped. She was a positive person, never focusing on the negative aspects of any situation. To find her in bed after my dad's appointment, fully dressed, with the shades drawn, hadn't been easy to see.

But it hadn't been easy to watch Daddy drive off either. It'd happened right after we walked out of the doctor's office.

We'd gotten to the parking lot, and he'd said, "Jesse, take your mother home. I need ... to go for a drive." Before I could utter a response, he was gone.

Mom didn't move from where she was standing. She

stayed frozen in the same spot, watching him drive away. Without her. Completely devastated.

I'd told her he needed time. It was the only thing that made sense since leaving his family after such a traumatic moment wasn't something he would ever normally do.

The truth was, we also needed time.

Time ... we didn't have.

"Yes, Mom?"

She was aching. She was in a state of shock. She'd wanted to tell the doctor he was wrong, that he needed to fix my father, and if he wasn't going to, then she would. That was what wives and mothers did—we fixed.

But it didn't matter what she said or tried. It would all be for nothing. This was one she couldn't solve and she couldn't fix.

It was the most helpless, heart-wrenching thing to watch.

"I'm scared." Her voice was so soft that I barely heard her.

I had to be the strong one. I had to hold the both of us up. One day, I would be able to fall apart, but that wasn't today.

"I'm here, Mom. We're going to get through this together."

"Please stay." She brought the wine up to her lips, so I did also. She swallowed several times, and I did the same. "I usually send you home to your husband and kids, but today, I need you."

"I'm not going anywhere," I assured her.

Remembering the photo I had seen on Dad's nightstand, I rolled back to grab it and set it on the bed between us. It was a framed picture of my parents on their wedding day. It had a dull finish, which was popular back then, and round corners. Mom's dress was simple despite the decade, but her hair made up for it.

As she stared at the picture in my hands, her eyes dripped with tears. Her lips quivered. Her body shook like she had a fever. "God help us," she whispered.

She went into the bathroom before I had the chance to try to comfort her. The door shut and locked. With the silence in her bedroom, I could hear everything. I expected a sob she could no longer hold back or the sound of her blowing her nose.

What I hadn't expected was to hear her throwing up.

TWENTY-ONE

JESSE

AFTER

"MOM, CAN I TALK TO YOU?" Viv said from the doorway of the library.

I'd been watching the clock, waiting to see how long it would take her to come and see me. "Of course, baby."

I watched her walk in, wearing skinny jeans and a long sweater, the neck wide and hanging well past her shoulder so that her bra strap was exposed. If Emery saw it, he'd tell her to change. My opinion was, I liked the way it looked. She had beautiful shoulders, and there was no reason she shouldn't show them off when a bra wasn't any different than a bathing suit.

Emery and I could be in denial all we wanted, but our daughter was going to college next year. Showing a bra strap was the least of our worries.

What I really worried about was Viv in Boston. She knew the city; she'd been going there since she was a baby. She knew the hard work and determination it would take to maintain a

GPA that would please us. But, to really survive in that city, you needed an edge, and that was something she didn't have.

"I think Luz is upset with me," she said as she sat in the chair next to mine.

I had been afraid of this, but I didn't let her know that as I said, "Why would she be mad at you, honey?"

"When I came down for breakfast yesterday morning, she told me Dad had sent her a screenshot of my text to show how late we were up. I guess he was furious."

When we had been in one of the art galleries yesterday, Emery had told me he'd reached out to Luz. I wasn't happy he'd done that, but there was nothing I could do. I just had to wait to see what would happen.

Turned out, I hadn't had to wait for long.

"Mom, I don't get why Dad's mad." She wrapped her arms around her stomach, her voice telling me how upset she was. "When Luz came to check on us, I told her we were still awake because you'd said we could stay up. Now, Dad's pissed, and Luz thinks I lied. This whole time, I thought I was doing the right thing because you'd told me it was all right."

"Don't worry."

"But I didn't lie, Mom. You know that."

My daughter wasn't a liar. She also wasn't sensitive. But her integrity was at play, and that was what was affecting her right now. I had to be careful. I didn't want her to discuss any of this with Emery. I needed her to believe I would dissolve whatever Luz was feeling and that this whole thing could be forgotten.

"Do you trust me?" I reached forward, gently lifting the large chunk of hair that had been resting on her shoulder and running my fingers through it.

"Of course."

"Then, know that I'll take care of this. You have nothing to worry about. Luz will not be upset with you after I speak to her." Finishing, I tucked the hair behind her ear. "So, don't think about it for another second." The longer the topic stayed open, the more questions she would ask, so I said, "Did you guys have fun with Charlotte?"

She shrugged. "We went to some pottery place and made a bunch of planters for Dad. Picked up a pizza on our way home, and we watched a movie."

I smiled. Viv just couldn't see it. "What's the planter look like?"

She pulled all of her hair to one side and took out her phone to show me a picture. "Dad's going to love it. See how it's geometric and super angular and short." She was flipping through several different shots now. "I painted mine an eggplant color; it's just hard to tell in the light."

She had been Daddy's girl from the moment she was born, and I never had a problem with it. I loved seeing how sensitive Emery was with her and the way she idolized him.

When her father and I had been dating and first gotten married, I always pictured him with a son, never a daughter. Then, I'd watched him take Viv out of my arms at the hospital and immediately soften with her. She'd owned him from that moment on.

"Sounds like it was a good night then?" I asked.

"It was all right." She pulled her phone away and set it on the chair, bending her knees and curling her toes around the edge of the cushion.

Viv wasn't overly enthusiastic about anything unless she

was talking about design, her friends, or boys. That was when I couldn't get her to stop talking.

My sweet girl.

It just meant I had to push a little more. "I'm just curious if you thought she was cool or not."

She rolled her eyes. "I'm not really sure why it matters, but yeah, she was okay. I liked the music she listened to in the car. She didn't lecture us when we got soda at the pizza shop. She let us use paper plates instead of the real ones and didn't make us wash the glasses." She dropped her legs and stood. She was done. "Is there anything else you want to ask me?"

"No, baby. You can go."

She began to walk out of the library but stopped when she reached the doorway. "I think I'm going to go over to Trever's house."

It took a minute for me to remember Trever was the new kid who had transferred to her school. The guy she had gone on a date with, who she was still texting with every night.

"Are Trever's parents home?" I asked.

"No."

I hated this part of parenting, knowing everything I did and every decision I made would affect her.

She could have gone to his house after school and told me she was at a girlfriend's. She could have told me his parents were home. She hadn't had to tell me the truth.

But she had, and I trusted her. I'd raised her to know what was right. She wouldn't just go to any boy's house. This one had to be special.

"Be home for dinner," I told her.

She smiled long enough to show me that my answer pleased her.

"Viv," I said, stopping her before she reached the door, "make smart choices."

She knew what that meant. She'd been hearing me say it to her since she was a kid. And, despite trusting her, I was still her mom, and I still needed to remind her.

"Always," she replied, and then she was gone.

It would only take a phone call to one of the other parents at Viv's school, and I could get everything I'd ever need to know on Trever and his family. I wasn't going to do that, nor was I going to focus on what might happen at Trever's house. Instead, I was going to send Luz a text to fix the disaster Emery had created.

I took out my phone, opened the last message I'd sent her, and began to type.

Luz: Their bedtime was a miscommunication between my daughter and me, but she did not lie to you. When Emery reached out, he didn't understand the circumstances and reacted unfairly. I'm sorry for all of it, Luz. Please accept my apology, and please don't be upset with Viv. This isn't her fault.

An anxiousness entered my chest as I reread the words I'd sent her. It wasn't in my character at all to do something like I had done a few days ago when I told my daughter she could stay up late.

One day, it would all make sense.

I believed that.

I set my phone on the table, and the movement caused my heart to race. It felt as though I'd just returned from a run. The reality was that I hadn't gone on one in months.

The hands were back, circling my throat, cutting off my air so that none was passing into my lungs.

My brain was racing.

What if I stop breathing? What if I have to go to the hospital?

What if Emery goes with me?

I had to clear my head. I had to loosen the grip from around my throat.

I had to find air again.

But, just as I started to stand, to walk over to the tall bookcase where I'd run my fingers over the spines, I saw an e-mail come through my laptop. It was from Charlotte, who was in the office down the hall with my husband, giving me their schedule for next week. They were going to be traveling to Boston on Wednesday morning and returning Friday evening.

Suddenly, the air was back in my lungs.

I walked into my bedroom, changed into a pair of compression pants, a fleece, and a headband made of the same material. Then, I put on a pair of sneakers and stopped in the kitchen to get some water. Emery was standing in front of the open fridge, staring at the shelves.

I wrapped my arms around his waist. "Can I help?"

"I'm trying to figure out what I want."

"Luz made some fresh salsa this morning, and there are chips in the pantry."

His hands went to mine, and he squeezed them. "That sounds good." He turned his head, and I felt his eyes on me, looking up and down my body. "Where are you going?"

I pressed my face into his back, hugging him from behind, and said, "For a run."

TWENTY-TWO
CHARLOTTE

CHARLOTTE HAD NEVER HEARD THE BLACKS' house this quiet before. But, with Jesse at her mother's, Viv at a study group, and Tommy at a friend's, that only left her and Emery, and the two of them had been working nonstop for hours, not muttering a single word between them.

It had been a stressful day. Emery's team was strong, and they could handle a significant workload, but nothing had gone right from the moment Charlotte arrived at ten minutes of nine this morning. With all the disasters she'd been dealing with, she'd really started to learn the intricate layers of Emery's business, becoming knowledgeable in environmental reports and soil testing and wind mitigation—things she had known nothing about before. And, surprisingly, Charlotte was really enjoying it. She liked knowing how much she was helping him and how much work she was taking off his plate the most.

Tonight was going to be a late evening. Emery had a set of drawings due at midnight, so Charlotte was acting as a filter, making sure no one got through to her boss, giving him the space he needed to finish. But, if she wanted to last any longer, she needed to put some food in her body.

She stood, stretching her arms and back before she walked to the kitchen. She roamed the shelves of the fridge, grabbing a package of freshly sliced turkey. She took out two baguettes from the bread basket, added in the meat, and covered it with cranberry relish and Brie, and then she toasted the sandwiches. She added some cucumber salad to the plate and brought them into Emery's office with silverware and napkins.

She said nothing as she set the dish in front of him and the other on her desk, returning to the kitchen for drinks. She made Emery's favorite, which was seltzer with a splash of cranberry and lime, and got water for herself, placing his on his coaster.

By the time she sat down, she heard, "Charlotte, this is excellent."

"Oh." She blushed. She hadn't expected such a response. She was even a little surprised he had looked up from his computer since he had been in such a zone today. "I'm glad you like it."

"I don't think I've eaten all day."

"You haven't."

Charlotte hadn't either. Neither of them had moved unless it was to use the restroom in the far side of the office, and Emery hadn't even done that.

She bit into her sandwich just as he said, "I appreciate you making me dinner."

She nodded, covering her mouth when she replied, "I'm a professional sandwich maker."

"Why sandwiches?" He wiped his lips with the napkin, placing it right back on his lap. "You're excellent at it; don't get me wrong. I just wonder why you didn't choose something like pasta or cheesecake."

Charlotte took a drink. "I get a little passionate when it comes to baking bread, and sandwiches are the easiest dinners to make when you're single. Whatever fits between the slices is the perfect amount for one."

Once she took a breath, she realized what she had just said. She wasn't sure if telling her boss she was single was technically appropriate. She'd never discussed her relationship status with any of her managers before, but she had also never worked this closely with them. The proximity made things feel different, and giving him that information hadn't necessarily felt wrong.

Emery put a cucumber into his mouth and said, "I need to hear more about this bread-making."

Charlotte felt herself smile. This was something she loved talking about. She'd been baking bread since she was young. The ingredients weren't that expensive, and having it on hand meant she and her sister always had something to eat, which was important when growing up with a mother like theirs. Even though their mom worked at a gas station and Charlotte reminded her to bring home food, her mother never remembered. At least, that was the excuse she had given; however, she'd never forgotten beer.

Charlotte looked up from her desk, not realizing she had been staring at it. "I enjoy making all different kinds. Sometimes as simple as a white bread or a honey wheat. Even the sweeter ones, like pumpkin and banana. I find it relaxing."

At her previous job, she used to bring in treats for her coworkers. She'd do it a few times a month when she was experimenting with recipes, using them as guinea pigs. There was no reason she couldn't do the same at this job. She was sure the kids would enjoy it if she brought them something with chocolate chips. Since Emery and Jesse were on the healthier side, she was thinking a zucchini or an apple bran for them.

She decided not to mention it to Emery. She didn't want to set any expectations. But, if she had time over the weekend after returning from Boston, she would bring in a few loaves on Monday morning for everyone to enjoy.

"You've been doing it for a while?" he asked.

Charlotte nodded with a huge piece of turkey in her mouth. "Long enough." She swallowed and leaned into her desk, dragging a cucumber through the dressing. "Can I ask you something?"

"Sure."

"I know, tomorrow, we'll be flying on a smaller plane. Will it feel similar to the commercial one we took?"

Emery used the seltzer to wash down whatever was in his mouth, and then he wiped his lips with his napkin. "You don't like to fly?"

He had read her expression wrong. She didn't want him to think she feared the flights they would be taking weekly, therefore dreading the trips to Boston, because that wasn't the case. She just didn't have a lot of experience flying and didn't know what to expect out of a smaller plane.

"Don't love it. Don't hate it either. I've certainly never flown private before, so I don't know if it's different."

"It's different all right." He moved several cucumbers around on his plate before he put them in his mouth. "A lot less people, a lot more luxury. The process will take two hours door to door instead of five."

"Sounds lovely."

Emery smiled, and Charlotte found herself staring at it.

"As for the flight, it'll be about the same. The plane will be much smaller, but if the air is rough, it doesn't matter what size jet you're in; you're going to feel it."

Charlotte had read the brochures on both companies he had been considering. Each had given her about the same information Emery just had. She still thought it was reassuring to hear it from him, and now, maybe she wouldn't be so nervous for tomorrow's flight.

Knowing their time together was limited before he shut her off to design again, she lifted her tablet off the desk and pressed the screen. "Can we just take a second to confirm your schedule for Boston?"

He started on the second half of his sandwich, swallowing before he said, "We're going straight to the jobsite after we land where we'll be meeting the builder. Once we get everything done there, we'll go to my house where we'll meet Adam and work the rest of the day."

Charlotte glanced between the screen and Emery, making sure she had allocated the right amount of time to work with his plan.

"As you know, Wednesday night, the builder and I will be having dinner with the mayor of Boston." Emery paused, so Charlotte glanced at him. "I would like you to come," he said.

"Really?" She couldn't contain her excitement. She had made the reservation for them at the highest-rated restaurant in Boston. While doing so, she'd taken a peek at the menu just to see how delicious it looked, never expecting she would be ordering from it.

"I'll take that as a yes?"

Charlotte nodded. "Yes, thank you. I would love to attend."

Emery set his fork on top of his plate and pushed it to the side of his desk. He only had five hours until the designs were due, and as she'd learned his process, she had a feeling he would need every minute to finish.

She went over and picked up his dish, stopping in front of him long enough to say, "Let me know if I can get you something or do anything to help you. I'm going to stay until you're done."

"Thanks, Charlotte."

He turned toward his computer, hands now on the keyboard, eyes fixed on the screen. Within seconds, Emery was lost in a creative bubble. Charlotte didn't understand that process or what it felt like to be consumed by artistic energy. But, once she returned from the kitchen, where she'd cleaned up the counter and washed both of their dishes, she watched Emery. She followed his hands and the images he was making on the screen. She was amazed at what she was seeing.

The more time she spent staring at him, the more she began to understand this talent he had. She just couldn't believe his level of focus. It was as though he didn't know she was even in the room.

Charlotte couldn't forget he was here.

And that wasn't just because he was her boss.

TWENTY-THREE
JESSE
BEFORE

WHEN I SHOULD HAVE BEEN at work, when I should have been home with my family, I found myself parked in the lot with the three brick buildings, the library the one in the middle. While the engine ran, my hands gripped the steering wheel as I braced myself for the guilt. It started at the back of my throat, eating its way through the rest of my body like a foundation full of termites.

My kids deserved this time with me.

My husband.

Why am I here?

I couldn't answer that. But it had been three days since I was here last, and I hadn't been able to stop thinking about this place. Something in that library was calling to me, and I had no idea what it was.

I grabbed my purse and climbed out of the driver's seat. As I walked in, there was an older gentleman sitting at the front desk. We saw each other at the same time.

"Hello," he greeted me.

I moved closer, not needing to look at his name tag when I said, "Good morning, Gregory."

I wasn't going to apologize. Bay had said I didn't need to. I still wanted to acknowledge him, which was the opposite of what I had done the last time he saw me.

"Morning," he replied.

I reached my hand in his direction. "I'm Jesse."

"Nice to meet you." I slowly pulled my fingers away, and he continued, "Enjoy yourself today."

I thanked him and moved deeper into the stacks. I took the same approach as last time, not heading in a specific direction, just wandering the aisles, catching titles that didn't look familiar. Within a few rows, I came across a dull teal cover that had gold lettering on the spine with flowers etched into the thick, heavy binding.

I didn't know what genre I was in, nor did I recognize the title, but I lifted it off the shelf and brought it over to a chair, opening to the first page.

I wasn't more than a few paragraphs in when I heard, "You're back."

I looked up, and Bay was standing only a few feet away.

I shrugged. "Apparently, I just can't stay away."

She sat across from me, staying at the very edge of her seat. "How have you been, Jesse?"

I went into my purse, grabbed the book I had borrowed, and set it on the table between us. "It was excellent."

A grin filled her whole face. "I was hoping you'd read it. Tell me what you loved about it."

My eyes fell to the cover as I remembered the story inside and the journey it had taken me on from the moment I opened it. "The voice of the heroine." When I glanced back up, there was a warmth in Bay's stare. It made me not want to look away again. "I immediately fell for her tone. At eighty-two, she was confident from a lifetime of experiences and so wise. I'm envious of her knowledge."

She turned her head as though she were intrigued by my answer. "Were you expecting the granddaughter to be the villain?"

I crossed my legs, wincing for a second. "You know, I thought it was the daughter up until the very end. The granddaughter came as a total surprise."

"Same." I didn't think her smile could get larger, but it did. "What's next on the to-be-read pile?"

"What's ..." My voice trailed off. I needed to get a little personal with her again. "I haven't been reading, which is so out of character for me because it used to be one of my favorite things to do. But, when Dad got sick, it started to feel like a chore, just another thing that wanted something from me."

"It lost its purpose."

I thought about what she'd said, unable to describe it any better. "Exactly."

"That can happen. We go through phases. There are certain things I didn't like when I was younger that I love now."

"Like?"

"Tomatoes. I thought they were the vilest vegetable when the fast-food restaurants would put thick slices of them on my hamburgers. To make it even worse, when I took the tomato off, it'd take all the mayo with it and leave behind all its seeds."

I laughed. Tommy also hated tomatoes, and the same thing had happened to me on more than one occasion. "I can relate on so many levels."

"But I love tomatoes now, just like your love of reading has finally returned to you."

I squeezed the new book in my hands. "Do you know this one?"

Bay held out her hand. "May I?"

I gave her the hardcover, and she gazed at both sides. "I haven't read it. Haven't even heard of it actually."

"I love the cover."

"It's happiness." She set the book on the table beside the one I had borrowed, which had a much more somber theme. "Especially in comparison to the darker one you just finished."

"I agree." I tightened my arms around my stomach. I wasn't sure why this question made me nervous. I was sure she was asked it all the time. "Would you suggest a book for me to read?"

Her grin caused my own lips to tug at the corners. "I'd be honored." She stood and said, "I'll go get the one I'm thinking of. I'll be right back."

Normally, this was the moment when I reached into my purse and took out my phone, checking my messages until she returned. I didn't want to do that. I didn't even have the smallest desire to peek at the screen.

The library had become my happy place. Once inside, I wouldn't feel guilty for not spending these hours with my kids. I would come in here and shut it all off, escaping, avoiding the reality of what was happening outside those double doors. I wouldn't tell anyone about my time here—not my husband, kids, or my friends.

The time I spent here was just for me.

So, rather than go for my phone, I unraveled my arms and rested them on the armrests, pushing myself back into the seat.

As I glanced around, I took in the smell of books and watched the students move throughout the room and listened to the conversations happening around me. Knowing the direction she had gone in, I continued to look toward it, waiting for her to round the corner. When she did, she was holding a large brown hardback. She gave it to me before she returned to her seat.

It was so old; I could barely read the title, eventually figuring out it said, *Tumbling Down*. The fragrance was intense, as though the entire smell of the library had been marinating on the pages for years.

"What is it?" I asked when I finally glanced up.

"A little gem I found when I first started working here. Not a single person has checked it out in all that time."

I opened the front cover and felt the grittiness of the aged paper. "If I enjoy it, I'll let my girlfriends know, and they'll come here and check it out. It will become your most requested title."

She held out her hand. "Give it back for a sec." When the book was in her grasp, she told me she would be just a minute, and she disappeared behind one of the stacks. I had no idea what she was up to or where she had gone, but when she returned, she placed the book in my lap and said, "Keep it. It's yours."

I glanced down, staring at the heaviness of it, and then back up at her. "I can't do that."

"I promise, it won't be missed."

"You're sure?"

"Please, Jesse, take it. It would mean everything to me to know you and your friends are enjoying this book rather than it just sit here and get no love."

I wanted to finish the one with the gorgeous teal cover first, and then I would start the brown hardcover. It wouldn't take more than four days to complete both.

"The next time I see you, I want a full report," she said.

"Deal."

I even knew who I'd lend the book to next. Alicia was always sending out texts, asking for reading recommendations. If this was as good as I hoped, then I had the first reader already lined up.

She was still standing but had taken a few steps back from me. "How's your dad doing?"

I sighed, shaking my head. "He still has okay days. Not great, but enough."

She didn't need to say a word. I saw the sympathy in her eyes, and that was without her even knowing what was wrong with my father.

"Thank you for asking," I added.

She gave me a small wave. "I'll see you soon, Jesse."

Once she was gone, I slipped Bay's book into my bag and opened up the teal one again, flipping to the first page. The second I fell back into the words, I was lost.

TWENTY-FOUR
JESSE
AFTER

"WHAT'S FOR DINNER?" Tommy said as he came strolling over to the counter.

Once the kids had come home from school, I'd sent them to their rooms to finish their homework, so their night would be free. It was our first evening without Emery, and I had every second of it planned until it was time for them to go to bed.

I smiled, anticipating his reaction. "Stuffed shells."

"Yes!"

I waved him over. "Come here."

As soon as he reached me, he wrapped his arms around my waist, and I pressed my lips to the top of his head, inhaling his scent. We stood just like that—my fingers clutching a spatula, the timer going off on the oven, my phone beeping with a message. None of it mattered, only him.

He gave me three beats; that was it, and then the moment was over.

But, right before I pulled my lips away, I said, "Go set the table and fill the glasses with ice and water. Dinner is going to be ready in five minutes."

He groaned a little, eventually heading toward the cabinet that held the plates. In the meantime, I ignored all the notifications on my screen and sent Viv a text, telling her to come downstairs to eat. Leaving my phone on the counter, I grabbed the pot holders and took out the shells.

This was a meal Emery and the kids had loved from the very first time I made it. I'd worked so much that I never had time to cook, so they all considered it a treat when I did. Since work was no longer a problem, I thought this would be a good night to serve it.

I put the salad I'd made into three bowls and brought those along with the casserole dish to the table. It took two trips, but by the time I was done, Tommy was, too, and Viv was just taking a seat.

"Oh yes, it's shells night," she said when she saw what I was scooping onto the plates.

I handed each of them dishes and passed the garlic bread.

"*Mmm*," Viv groaned. "I had this last week at Trever's house, and it didn't even compare to yours, Mom."

Trever, the boy she had gone to see when his parents weren't there. The one she had done nothing with because I had seen it all over her face when she returned home for dinner.

We'd raised unbelievable children.

"Mom," Tommy said, looking up from his plate, "I've missed your cooking so much."

"I've missed it, too," I admitted. It wasn't that I loved my time in the kitchen. It was knowing that I was feeding them something good, that I was giving them a meal they would enjoy. That was the rewarding part about cooking.

"Now that you're home, I say you make this once a week," Viv said.

I covered my mouth after a bite. "I'm sure I can arrange that."

"Sometime soon, you're going to have to teach me how to do it all," she continued. I stared at my daughter, trying to piece together what she was saying. "Since there's going to be a kitchen in the basement of our dorm, if I ever get the chance to go grocery shopping, I want to know how to make something."

Oh God.

My little girl.

Once she was gone, she'd never come back. I hadn't. I'd stayed in Boston every summer between school years, not wanting to return to the quiet town in Maine where I was from. Viv would crave the city once she spent a few weeks there. Vermont would become far too still for her.

I wondered how her father would handle that.

I shivered at the thought and said, "The next time Dad goes to Boston, let's do a cooking night. We'll go to the store and get the ingredients, so you're comfortable with that part, and then we'll make it together. How does that sound?"

"Sounds fun," she replied.

"What's planned for tonight?" Tommy asked.

I'd thought a lot about how I wanted to spend my first night home alone with them. I'd considered taking them sledding or ice skating, shopping or to the movies—all things they loved. Instead, I'd chosen something we hadn't done in a long time—at least, not the way I was going to suggest it.

I set down my fork, my stare moving between theirs. "I thought we could go in the Jacuzzi."

Tommy's head turned in Viv's direction and then back at me. "Don't even tell me you want to go snow-dipping?"

Emery had built our Jacuzzi on the back deck that overlooked the mountains. Off that large space was a set of stairs that led to the backyard. In the winter, when the kids were younger, we used to rush down the stairs and dive into the massive snow banks. Once our skin turned raw and red, we would rush back up the stairs and climb into the hot tub, burning from the difference in temperature. As they got older, they began to do it with their friends. It had been a few years since either of them went hot-tubbing with us.

"Would you be up for it?" I asked them.

"Oh my God." Viv laughed. "If you're willing to jump, then, of course, we're up for it."

"I want to go right now," Tommy said, his fork clanking as he dropped it on the dish.

"Both of you need to finish your dinner." I took a bite of my garlic bread. "Once you're done, we'll clean up and rest for a little bit, and then it's on."

They laughed at my change in tone, two of the most beautiful faces staring back at me.

I could have been more creative with tonight's plans. Charlotte had brought the kids to a pottery class, and I wasn't even taking them out of the house. But I was spending time with them. Quality time. When I'd stepped back from Cinched, this right here was what I wanted.

I was finally getting it.

And it was perfect.

I grinned back at them. "I picked up dessert, too. I got everything to make sundaes."

"What's everything?" Viv asked.

I cut one of the shells into thirds and popped the first section into my mouth. "Oreo ice cream, hot fudge, whipped cream, and sprinkles."

"Wow," Tommy said, his expression causing me to laugh.

It was so easy to make them happy.

"Snow-dipping, shower, ice cream, bed," I informed them. "And maybe, just maybe, I'll make homemade French toast for breakfast before school tomorrow."

"*Yesss!*" Tommy shouted, and he began to dance.

Viv joined in, and I did, too. The three of us started to laugh, and we couldn't stop. My cheeks hurt, and my stomach ached. But I loved every second of it.

Because I was lost.

Again.

But, this time, it was with my kids.

TWENTY-FIVE
EMERY

EVERY TIME I walked into the builder's office, forty-two stories up in downtown Boston, the stress surrounding this project would thicken a little more. Today was no goddamn exception. Budgets were blown, timelines were thin, and tension was mounting. The builder wanted me to offer solutions.

I had none.

We were in it. Knee deep. And we were going to have to find a way to make it all work.

But, tonight, we had to back away from it all. We were going to get dressed up and break bread with the mayor.

We'd been so busy at the builder's office that we ended up staying much longer than I'd planned, and we'd had to leave in a rush. Charlotte hadn't had time to go back to her hotel to change and get ready for dinner. She had to do it at my house. While she was in the guest room, I was in the master, finishing up brushing my teeth.

At some point this evening, I needed to thank her. She'd done so well today. She was under a lot of pressure and hadn't cracked. Not once, and there were plenty of moments when it would have been appropriate. She took every order, solved every problem. Everyone in that office relied on her, and she delivered.

Jesse had chosen one hell of a candidate.

Several years ago, when my business had first started changing, was when I'd really needed someone like Charlotte. I'd put it off for a long time, not wanting anyone in my space or to take the time to train them. Now that 3 Stuart Street had been announced and work was exploding, I needed someone competent to handle what was coming in.

Charlotte wasn't just handling it; she was the only person holding it all together. With her help, I'd achieve everything I ever wanted.

I set my toothbrush in the holder and wiped my face with a towel, tightening the one that was wrapped around my waist as I walked over to the closet. I chose a pair of navy slacks and a striped button-down and tucked the shirt in with a belt. I looked at my options for shoes and wasn't sure if I should go with the brown or the black. I knew nothing about fashion. I always relied on my wife to pick these things out.

The same way I would right now.

I found my phone on the dresser and called Jesse. She didn't answer, and after four rings, I heard her voice mail. By the time she heard my message, I'd probably already be at the restaurant, so I hung up.

I wished she'd answered. I hadn't spoken to her all day, and I just wanted to hear her voice.

I missed her.

Sighing, I returned to the closet, staring at both pairs of shoes, still in the same predicament. I went with the brown ones, and once I finished getting ready, I headed downstairs to meet Charlotte in the kitchen. She was standing at the counter with her back to me, wearing a tight black dress that revealed the entire outline of her body. It stopped just below her knees and ended with heels that were several inches tall.

Every man in that restaurant would be staring at her tonight, including the two we were going to be eating with. I shook my head at that thought and said, "Charlotte," from the entryway of the kitchen.

She slowly turned around. The front of her dress was as tight as the back, the material traveling all the way up to her neck.

Every one of her curves was on display.

Jesus Christ.

"Hey, Emery. What's up?"

A few seconds passed before I spoke, "I've got to ask you something."

"Okay."

I pointed down. "Are the brown shoes all right, or should I change to black?"

I felt like a fool for asking, but this dinner was important. All the details mattered. And I had a feeling Charlotte was the kind of woman who enjoyed being asked those types of questions.

Just like my wife.

She smiled. "The brown would be my choice. You did good." She handed me my jacket, which she must have grabbed from the coat closet.

I took it and thanked her. I added, "Are you ready to go?"

She layered up at the same time, hooking her overnight bag across her shoulder. "Ready and starving. The driver is waiting for us outside. He's going to stay at the restaurant while we eat, and then he'll take you home. I'll hop in a taxi or something after dinner."

I locked the front door behind us and joined her on the steps. "No way," I said. "I'm not going to send you in a separate car and worry about you getting to the hotel. I'll take you there myself and make sure you get there safely."

She looked at me before we reached the SUV. "Okay."

The driver opened the door to the backseat, taking the bag from Charlotte's hand before she climbed inside. I slid in after her, and we immediately merged into the road. It would take us about fifteen minutes to get to the restaurant. It was on the other side of the city, and traffic was never light at this hour.

"What's Jesse up to tonight?" Charlotte asked after there had been silence for several blocks.

I'd been looking out the window. I shifted my body toward her. "Last I heard, she wanted to stay in and cook the kids dinner."

I took out my phone and saw there was a text from her on the screen. I hadn't heard it come in, although she'd sent it two minutes ago. It was a photo of Jess and the kids with tomato sauce on their faces from the stuffed shells she'd made. Each of them was in a different pose, grinning.

I couldn't remember the last time I'd seen my wife smile that hard.

It had been years.

"I'm sure the kids will really enjoy that," Charlotte replied.

Jesse needed those kids right now, and she needed to be

surrounded by their laughter. It was the only thing that was going to get her through losing her dad.

I looked up from the phone and said, "Not as much as Jesse will."

TWENTY-SIX
CHARLOTTE

THE MAYOR PUT his arms on the large, round table, leaned forward, and looked at Emery and the builder while he said, "I'm really excited about this project, gentlemen."

Three and a half hours was how long they had been sitting there, indulging on the nine courses that had been served. The sommelier had paired just as many wines, swapping out empty glasses for full ones. Charlotte was on the verge of slurring.

Still, the whole evening had unraveled perfectly.

Once Charlotte and Emery had arrived, they had been taken into a private dining room. That was what Charlotte had requested when she made the reservation, telling the receptionist who was in the party and their need for a more secluded space. The room they had been brought to was magnificent, lit only by candles. Everything on the table was mirrored and glass, causing the fiery reflection to shimmer off each surface.

"I knew you would be," the builder replied to the mayor. "A building with this prestige and exclusivity is exactly what the Back Bay needs."

The mayor looked at Emery and said, "I had been envisioning something in that space for a long time. I didn't want something too modern. I certainly wasn't looking for traditional. We need different but without a stark contrast, so the skyline weighs equally in every spot." The mayor twirled his glass on top of the table, causing the little wine that was left inside to swirl. "What you designed, Emery, is more than any of us could have ever imagined."

The mayor's wife nodded. So did the builder and his wife. They all gazed at Emery with so much adoration in their eyes. But none of them were smiling as hard as Charlotte. She might not have been there when he was designing the tower; however, she hadn't needed to be. She saw how hard her boss worked, how many hours he put in every day. It was inspiring and motivating and so incredibly sexy; she had thought that from the moment she saw him online. The wine just forced her to focus on it.

"Thank you," Emery responded.

They were the humblest two words Charlotte had ever heard.

The builder grabbed the top of Emery's arm and shook it, laughing with him, showing Emery how pleased he was with his performance. "The residents of Boston have no idea what's about to hit them. We're going to start the biggest bidding war this city has ever seen."

From what Charlotte had learned so far, Emery wouldn't be a part of that. His responsibility was solely the design of the structure and how to build it. Everything else, like the bidding war that could occur, had nothing to do with her boss. But, if that did happen, it would just be another accolade he could add to his growing list of accomplishments.

Charlotte was sure it would happen. This building was that special.

"Before we start arguing about price per square foot," the mayor said to the builder, "let's get to the more important question at hand." He wiped the corners of his mouth even though he'd finished eating over twenty minutes ago. "You're scheduled to break ground in exactly two months. I need to know if you're going to make that date." Before anyone had a chance to respond, he went on, "I know how these timelines work. What you have projected can be far from reality, and many factors come into play to get these babies off the ground." His stare slowly moved between the two men but settled on the builder. "I'm going to make things happen on my end—clearing permits, rerouting traffic, getting you fast inspections. But I need a date, and I need it to be set in stone."

Two months was what they had announced to the public. But Charlotte knew how much work needed to be done before construction could start. She and Emery had made a list when she first began working for him. It was extensive. She had been working her way through it, and there was still so much to do.

There were multiple pieces to this puzzle, and Charlotte was the first one.

Emery looked at her, and in his eyes was a question. He wanted to know if she could make the deadline.

They both knew it would be almost impossible. Three months was more reasonable. Four was still not enough, but it would give them much more room.

Emery didn't have four. He had two. And he needed a commitment from Charlotte, or the entire timeline would have to be adjusted.

Charlotte was taking a huge risk by giving him this answer.

She was already losing sleep; it would only get worse if she suddenly had a hard cutoff date in addition to the workload she was already carrying for Emery, so all of his focus could go on 3 Stuart Street.

It was going to be tight.

It was going to be a painful two months.

She was sure this could be the wine talking, but she opened her mouth and said, "I can make it happen on my end." By agreeing to the date, she was giving Emery, the builder, and the mayor her promise, and she didn't take that lightly.

Emery glanced at the builder, silently asking him the same question. Charlotte wasn't the only one who could hold things up. They each had responsibilities that were equally as challenging to complete.

Several seconds passed before Charlotte saw a slight nod of the builder's head.

"You have our commitment," Emery said to the mayor.

Charlotte immediately felt a rush inside her chest now that the date had been locked into place. For these two months, she decided she needed to focus only on her job, which meant the girls' night scheduled for next week was going to have to be canceled and the trip she was going to take her nieces on to Rhode Island would have to be postponed until spring.

Somehow, she'd get it all done.

She had to—for Emery and because she never went back on her word.

As though Emery could sense her anxiety, he gave her a calming look. It didn't help. The list of items that needed to be checked off wasn't getting any smaller while she was sitting here. She needed to get back to the hotel and open her laptop and fine-tune the list, coming up with a game plan to ensure everything got completed.

"I knew I could count on you boys," the mayor replied, sounding more than pleased. "And you," he said to Charlotte, "the bubbly little pulse behind it all." He filled his mouth with the rest of his wine and swallowed it in one gulp. "Now that we have that settled, I think it's time to call it a night."

Everyone stood and began to put on their coats. Charlotte did the same but struggled with her sleeve. She felt someone move in behind her and straighten it, making it easier to slip her arm through. When she turned around, she saw that it was Emery.

"Thank you," she said softly.

"I'm taking you to your hotel."

"You're sure?" Charlotte buttoned her jacket, starting at the bottom. She knew the hotel was close to his townhouse; she just didn't want to inconvenience him.

"Positive."

She wrapped her scarf around her neck, and the two of them said good-bye to the mayor and his wife, the builder and his. Then, they walked outside the restaurant to find the SUV.

Charlotte spotted it a few cars down and directed his eyes with her finger. "I think that's us over there."

Emery moved a little closer to her as he looked to where she was pointing. With only inches between them, she could feel the heat from his body. She could smell his cologne. She now knew what it was like to be within kissing distance of him.

It all made her ... hold her breath.

She wasn't sure how to process what this meant and why she'd been thinking about Emery more and more over the last few days. The only thing she did know was that she wasn't gazing at him the way an executive assistant should be looking at her boss.

"Yes, you're right," he said. Then, he was several feet away again, and he was holding his arm out, signaling for her to go first.

Air returned to her lungs as she pushed those thoughts far from her mind and moved toward the car. Emery stayed one step behind, just to the side of her, the same placement he always took whenever they walked together. Charlotte had learned that on the first day when they went into the kitchen at the same time. She'd never had a man take that position before. It felt protective, which was something else she'd never experienced.

She liked it.

"Did you have a good time tonight?" he asked as they weaved down the busy sidewalk.

She wanted to turn to him but didn't. "Yes, most definitely. It was the best meal I'd ever had." She finally looked at him. "The company was really wonderful, too. I loved getting the chance to meet the mayor."

"He seemed pretty taken with you."

Charlotte laughed, partly because she was filled with wine and actually found that funny and partly because she had no idea how to comment and this was much easier. "He's an interesting character."

"He's quite the bubbly pulse behind this city."

She laughed at Emery's description but didn't have the chance to say anything more as they reached the SUV.

The driver had seen them approach and gotten out,

opening the backseat door. Charlotte slid in, and Emery climbed in after.

"We'll need to stop at the hotel first," Charlotte said to the driver. She leaned back in her seat and glanced at Emery. She waited at least a block before she broke the silence. "Thank you for bringing me tonight."

"You're welcome." He rubbed his palm over his knee, glancing across the seat at her. "It's important for you to know him. We're going to be dealing with him during the whole project."

"I had a feeling."

"City politics can make things hard on a builder." His voice changed. "Boston has some heavy scar tissue we're going to have to get through before any ribbon-cutting ceremony takes place."

"I wondered that, too," she admitted. "Sounds like I have a lot to learn."

Emery shook his head. "You don't give yourself enough credit. I counted on you for an answer tonight, and you delivered, knowing it was going to be a hell of a deadline to meet." His hand stilled. "There will always be small things to learn. That never goes away. But, Charlotte, you're doing an excellent job."

She was grateful for how dark it was in the car, as it hid the redness in her cheeks.

Each of Emery's words repeated in Charlotte's head, and she basked in his compliments, appreciative for the recognition. It might have been a short amount of time, but she had been working hard.

And he had noticed.

That made her feel even more of his heat even though he wasn't touching her.

Since she didn't know how to reply, she softened her voice and gave him the truth. "It's been the most amazing experience, learning from you."

TWENTY-SEVEN
JESSE
AFTER

"EMERY, no! Don't let them. Don't let them do it!"

"Baby, wake up," I heard along with feeling my husband's hands shaking me.

My eyes flicked open. His face was the first thing I saw.

His lips came closer, gently pressing to mine, and the softest, "I'm home," whispered through them.

It took several seconds before I realized I had been napping in bed. Emery was lying next to me on his side, his arm bent with his palm supporting his cheek. *I'm home* meant he had returned from Boston, and according to the time, he hadn't been here for more than a few minutes.

"You were so beautiful. I didn't want to wake you," he said as my stare returned to him. "Until you started screaming ..." He put his hand on my cheek, rubbing it as though he were wiping tears, but my skin felt dry. "What were you dreaming about?"

It hadn't been a dream.

It had been a nightmare.

I thought everything through, filtering what I would say to Emery before I replied, "Daddy ... when they put him on the ventilator."

He pressed his lips to my forehead, holding them there when he said, "Get your mind off of it and tell me about your day."

That was such a good idea.

He could be so sweet.

"I took Tommy to school, went to the gym, got a massage, and climbed into bed to do some reading." I glanced back toward the nightstand, seeing that the book was there and my glasses were on top of it. I had fallen asleep with both, and Emery had taken them off.

My days had always looked so different from this.

This was going to be the new normal.

At least, for right now.

Oh God.

I took a breath and another, my airway starting to feel a little restricted, my heart beating so fast. "How did things go in Boston?"

His hand was underneath the blanket, moving to my navel, tracing small circles across it. "The mayor is going to get us everything we need. I just have to keep the builder and his team focused on construction instead of what the units are going to sell for."

"Good luck with that." I coughed, hoping it would loosen my throat, but it didn't help at all.

"I know." He shook his head. "I called you Wednesday night when I was getting ready to go out to dinner with him. I didn't know what color shoes to pair with my navy slacks, and you're usually there to tell me what to put on."

"What did you pick?"

"I went with the brown ones." He laughed, a smile spreading across his face as though he were remembering it. "I asked Charlotte her opinion, and those were the ones she chose. She has good taste."

I cleared my throat, not surprised the conversation had turned to her so quickly. "Sounds like she's still doing really well?"

"She's one of the best decisions we've made for my business."

It didn't matter how much anxiety was flowing through me; Emery needed to hear this.

I reached forward, placing my hand on his cheek, giving him every bit of love I could pull out of my pounding chest. "You have no idea how happy this makes me." My thumb swiped against his whiskers, feeling the roughness of each one. "I just had a gut feeling about her." I barely got the last part of the sentence out when the feelings inside of me began to intensify. They turned sharp, coming on faster, making me tighten from their strength. My fingers pressed into his cheek. My muscles contracting.

Oh God.

I was doing everything I could to hide this, to stop it from controlling me.

To stop it from winning.

It was always fucking winning.

My hand pulled away from him, but his was still on me, now moving to my thigh.

"What do you want to do tonight?" His fingers curved around to my hip and slid up to my ribs.

"I don't know."

Normally, his touch sent tingles through my body. Right now, with the war happening under my skin, it felt like needles.

I couldn't handle it.

"I think you said the kids were going to be gone for the night, so we can go downtown and grab a few drinks and ..."

The rottenness was growing. The tightening was increasing.

"Jess?"

He wanted something from me. An answer. I wasn't entirely sure how long he'd been waiting for one.

"Would you mind if we stayed in?" I pleaded. "Luz left us plates in the fridge. We can eat those and watch a movie or something. I'm just ... so tired."

I would do anything to get his eyes off me even if that meant fighting sleep during an action film that wouldn't hold my interest.

He sighed. "I don't mind at all. I have so much work to do." His touch turned lighter. "There's no need to reheat the plate. I ate on the plane."

He quickly kissed my forehead, and then he got off the bed. He went into his closet, and I could hear him changing out of his jeans and button-down. When he came out, he had on gray sweatpants and a Northeastern hoodie. The only thing he was missing was a hat. Then, I would have thought we were back in his dorm, and I was lying on his bottom bunk, watching him get ready for practice.

Those days. The ones before everything had started to hurt.

Oh God.

He came to my side of the bed, his hands going above my

head, his lips finding mine. "I'll be in my office if you need me."

I exhaled. It ached. It ached so hard. But I did it. "I missed you, Emery."

"You have no idea how much I missed you." He pulled away, and when he got to the door, he looked at me from over his shoulder. "No more nightmares, baby."

Once he left, I reached for my phone to distract myself from everything that was happening inside of me. If I focused on those thoughts and feelings, they would only get worse.

Worse would be intolerable.

I clicked on the pictures, flipping through every one. Most were of the kids. Lots were of Birdie. Randomly, I would come across ones of Emery and me. Our heads were pressed together, and he was smiling, showing teeth. Not me. Although my lips were pulled wide, they stayed shut, and my eyes were lifeless. In fact, I wouldn't call it a smile at all.

I went through two years of photos, desperate to find one where I was really grinning, my finger swiping the screen as fast as it could. I looked the same in each one.

When I'd seen enough, I opened the last text I'd sent to Bay, and I started typing.

Me: Do I smile?
Bay: Of course you do.
Me: But it doesn't really look like one. It doesn't even look like half of one. Or a quarter. And it never will again ... God, what happened to me?
Bay: None of us are what we used to be, Jesse. We're all changing.

I stared at her response. At the truth behind it. At the terrifying reality of how much my life had changed since even ... yesterday.

I needed happy—that was why I had texted her—so I brought up a subject both of us loved.

Me: I started the book you'd told me about last week. You're right, the passages in the diary are extremely harrowing.

I looked up from the phone, and my eyes fell onto our wedding photo that was sitting on my nightstand. That picture had been next to our bed since we got married, and it had moved with us to all the places we lived. The smile in that shot was nothing like the one I wore now.

It had dulled.

And I knew exactly when it'd happened.

Bay: I miss you.

Those three words were like a sledgehammer to my throat. Bay knew how much they affected me, and that was why she had sent them.

I set my phone down and rolled away from it.

It hurt too much to look at.

Everything hurt.

TWENTY-EIGHT
CHARLOTTE

CHARLOTTE HAD BEEN SITTING at the desk in her tiny living room, her hand on the mouse, several notebooks spread out in front of her for hours. She had multiple tabs open, flipping between projects to make sure each item that needed to get completed tonight would get an equal amount of attention. She'd even eaten in this spot, realizing she had left half of a tuna sandwich, two cherry tomatoes, and several pieces of rotini from the pasta salad she'd added to the plate. She had been so busy and forgotten, and now, the food had been sitting out too long to eat.

Getting up from her desk, she took the paper plate into the kitchen and dumped it in the trash. She grabbed a diet soda out of the fridge, and just as she was returning to the living room, her phone rang.

She looked at the screen and answered, "Emery?"

"Charlotte, you're awake. Hi. Shit …"

"Shit?"

"I didn't think you'd answer. I was prepared to leave a message, so I wouldn't forget what I had to tell you."

He could have texted a voice memo, but for some reason, Charlotte didn't point that out.

Instead, she said, "You're still working?"

She looked at the time. It was almost two in the morning. She couldn't believe it was that late and that she hadn't fallen asleep yet. And that Emery was going at it at this hour when he had a wife and two kids at home.

"I haven't stopped since I walked in the door," he said.

"Same here." Charlotte heard the rustling of paper. "What is it that you wanted to tell me?" She was holding a pen and one of the notebooks, ready.

A few seconds passed, and then he laughed. "I'm so tired; I forgot."

Charlotte laughed, too. She was delirious. She was positive she'd have to redo whatever she'd touched at this point. Therefore, she needed to focus on things that didn't challenge her brain, like organizing Emery's e-mail. "Is it about Boston?" She yawned. "Or the drawings for Ricco's Cape house? Or ..."

More silence until finally, "It's gone. I have no idea what it was."

"Happens to me all the time."

"I'm sorry for calling you so late."

Before Charlotte went into her bedroom, she set the notebook and pen back on the desk and flipped off the living room light. "Please, it's my job. I'll answer anytime you call."

Emery didn't understand Charlotte yet. He didn't know that, when she gave her commitment, like she had done the other night when having dinner with the mayor, she didn't go back on her word. Not answering her phone would be going against the promise she'd made to the Blacks when she accepted their offer of employment.

"I appreciate it," he replied.

"Of course." She took a drink of her soda. "Emery, I need you functioning on Monday morning, so try to get at least a little sleep this weekend." She felt the need to remind him because, without Emery, this project couldn't operate, and the builder couldn't survive without him.

"You'd better take your own advice."

Charlotte lifted her tablet off the nightstand, entered her password, and began to go through Emery's e-mails, filtering the ones he needed to see. It was a task she should have done days ago, but smaller things were slipping through the cracks with their new two-month deadline.

"I'm going right now," she said.

"If something else comes up or if I remember what I needed to tell you, would it be all right if I called tomorrow? I don't want to bother you on the weekends, but—"

"You're no bother, I assure you. Please call anytime."

"Good night, Charlotte," he said and hung up.

She set her phone down and pulled the blanket up to her chin, continuing to scroll through the large backlog of messages. She hadn't gotten through more than a few hundred when a text from Emery came across the screen of her phone.

Emery: I see you in my inbox. Go to bed.

Charlotte laughed when she saw she had been caught, but she was happy it had happened. As far as she knew, he had never questioned her dedication to this job. After tonight, she hoped he never would because she didn't know any other way to show him how committed she was.

She replied with a smile emoji, and then she put down her tablet and fell asleep.

TWENTY-NINE
JESSE
BEFORE

"HEY, JESSE," Bay said as she took a seat beside me in her own oversize leather chair. She crossed her legs, setting several folders on top of them. "I have a strange suspicion you finished both books."

I put in a bookmark and closed the hardcover I was holding. "I did."

"What did you think of *Tumbling Down*?"

"Oh, Bay."

She leaned her back into the side of the chair, shifting her body more toward me. "You fell madly, deeply in love with it, didn't you?"

I nodded, grinning. "Honestly, I wasn't prepared for how beautiful the words were going to be." I sighed, thinking of the storyline. It was a book I planned to read again the second I got it back from Alicia. "It was stunning from beginning to end."

"I knew you'd love it."

My fingers clung around the edge of the book as I felt the

heat move across my face. My cheeks were turning red; I couldn't help it. "Thank you for the inscription. I was so touched by it."

I had been so surprised to find the small note she had written on the inside of the cover, which was why she had asked for the book back after she gave it to me in the library. Since it was one of her favorites, in the most beautiful handwriting, she'd wished me a lifetime of enjoyment with the novel.

It was the sweetest gesture.

"It's my pleasure," she said, smiling. She glanced at the hardcover in my lap. "What about the other book you checked out? The one with the happy blue cover?"

Tumbling Down read almost like a classic. The kind of story everyone should finish just to appreciate the beauty of the written word. It had delicate descriptions and a prose style. I'd found myself savoring paragraphs to make it last longer.

The teal-covered book had a very different storyline that made me ache, just thinking about it. It was about courage and survival and the ugliness of life. I wouldn't be able to give the story justice if I described it to Bay. She had to experience it for herself.

"It was heavy," I told her. "Actually, it might be one of the most emotionally taxing books I've ever read."

Her eyes narrowed. "Tell me more. I'm intrigued."

I thought of an angle I could explain to her or a character I could describe without blowing the twist. There just wasn't one. "It's one of those books where, if I say anything, it will ruin everything for you. It's best to go in completely blind."

"Sold. I have to read it." She moved positions, switching

the way her legs were crossed. "Hey, before I forget to ask, how's Dad doing?"

Every time she asked me that, she blew my mind.

I shrugged, shaking my head. "Today hasn't been a good day at all."

"What happened?"

"He has a trach, and it caused an infection, which means another hospital stay, more antibiotics, more confusion when he gets released and goes back home."

Pity filled her eyes like it had the first time we talked about him. "Is your mom still alive?"

"She is. They've been married since they were eighteen." I thought about the sound of her voice this morning when she'd told me Dad was getting admitted. "She's the strongest woman I know."

She reached across and put her hand on mine, and that was when I realized I was now gripping the armrest. "Something tells me you got your strength from her."

"I'm not sure about that."

So much warmth went into her smile when she said, "It's just a hunch I have."

"Thank you." My voice was just a little above a whisper. Her eyes told me she'd heard it. "It's great, seeing you again, Bay."

"You, too, Jesse." She released me and stood and took a few steps. "Will you be back soon?"

"Very soon."

She waved and walked away, and I reopened the book in my lap. The description promised a light story, and that was exactly what I needed after the two I just finished.

I was only about a chapter in when I realized I'd forgotten

to give Bay the title of the teal book. I'd already returned it, so I didn't have it in my bag to give to her. I was sure she could get the name by tracking me down in their system and seeing what I'd checked out. But something told me she wouldn't do that. She'd wait and ask me the next time she saw me. And, at this rate, that would be only in a few days.

THIRTY
CHARLOTTE

CHARLOTTE USED her key to enter through the front door of the Blacks' townhouse. Unlike their place in Vermont, this one didn't have a code, but it was just as spectacular. This house was actually Charlotte's favorite out of the two. She liked the height of the ceilings and the little details she'd never seen in any other home and the textures that had been used throughout.

She also really loved Boston, a place she hadn't ever considered moving to until she'd been offered this job.

She shut the front door behind her and went into the kitchen. Marion was at the counter, cutting up fresh fruit.

"Good morning," Charlotte said to her, continuing to the coffeemaker, hitting the buttons to pour a single cup. She had walked from the hotel, and even though it wasn't far, she could feel the chill all the way in her bones.

"Morning, Miss Charlotte," she replied. "I gave Mr. Black his coffee when he came down in his pajamas about an hour ago."

"Thank you," Charlotte answered. She brought the mug over to the fridge where she added in some creamer. "Is Adam here yet?"

"No, just Mr. Black."

Charlotte pointed up, letting Marion know where she was headed, and she moved over to the stairs. As she started to climb them, she heard Emery. It sounded like he was on the phone, and by the tone of his voice, he wasn't pleased.

"The measurements are perfect," he snapped. "There isn't a doubt in my mind."

She was halfway up and could hear him more clearly now.

"I don't give a shit what your foreman told you," Emery said. "Those measurements haven't changed." He paused. "I stand by my word."

When Charlotte reached the top of the stairwell, she saw Emery in the doorway of his bedroom. The only thing covering his body was a small white towel wrapped around his waist.

"This is bullshit," he said.

Charlotte was frozen on the top step, eyes glued to her boss's back, overly impressed with how muscular and fit he looked. Her stare slowly dipped all the way to his feet, and then she forced herself to glance away and start walking toward the office.

But, within a step, Emery heard her and turned around.

Their eyes locked.

She tried so hard not to look down, especially because he would know what she was doing. But she couldn't fight it ... and his whole body came into view.

Every edge.

Every dip of muscle.

There was a perfect amount of hair on his chest and a thin

trail that disappeared under the towel. There were droplets of water still on his skin, his hair messy, like someone had been gripping it.

Emery Black was so incredibly sexy.

"I told you the numbers," he growled, startling her. "I'm not going to tell you again."

Their eyes caught one last time, and he disconnected the call.

Charlotte opened her mouth to say something, anything to make this situation less awkward and to cool him down from the argument.

But he didn't give her the chance.

He immediately turned and shut the door.

Her heart was beating so fast by the time she reached the office; it felt like she had climbed ten sets of stairs. Her hands were shaking as she took a seat at her desk and pulled up her e-mail. She tried to focus on what needed to be done, but all she could see was Emery's body. She was so distracted by it that, when Adam walked into the office, she jumped.

"Morning," he said, chuckling at her. He took off his cross-body bag and set it on his desk. "Too much coffee?"

She pointed at the mug on her desk and exaggerated, "Fourth cup."

"Sounds about right."

She swiveled her chair to get a better view of the door. "Any idea what pissed off the builder this morning? At least, I'm assuming it was him. I've never heard Emery argue with anyone else."

He took a seat, and his fingers began tapping the keyboard. "I'm sure it was him. That dude is fucking crazy. I guess, if I had that many millions invested in a project, I'd be that crazy, too. Were they really going at it?"

Before she could answer him, her phone dinged, and a text popped up on the screen. Adam's cell went off at the same time, and the both of them read the group message from Emery.

Emery: Going for a run. Be back in an hour. Don't call unless it's an emergency.

"He's definitely pissed," Adam said as he glanced at Charlotte. "I've never known him to miss a meeting."

The three of them were supposed to be at the builder's office in an hour. If Emery was just returning by then, they would be lucky if they got there an hour late.

Charlotte couldn't let that happen.

She needed to fix this.

THIRTY-ONE
EMERY

"TELL ME THIS IS WORTH IT," I said to Jesse when she answered the phone.

Over two miles, and I didn't feel any better. I still wanted to get in that bastard's face and tell him how I really felt. I had known this project was going to be hard, and he had a reputation for being an asshole, but I hadn't known he was going to make me this angry.

"This is only temporary," she replied. "I want you to take a deep breath and remember why you're doing this and how much you love what you do and how you're changing the skyline of the city where we met."

She was right.

But that was why I had called my wife. I didn't even have to tell her what had gotten me so worked up. She always just knew what I needed and what to say to make me feel right again. And, in this case, she knew what to do to stop me from exploding.

I sighed. "Jess, I almost lost it on him. I was that close to snapping."

"Whether he deserved it or not, that's not you, and it's not how you do business."

I ran my hand through my hair, feeling the beads of sweat fall onto my neck. "You're right again."

"Listen to me, Emery. This is stressful, but you're doing an amazing job at handling it all. You have a solid team, tons of support, and a family who thinks you're a hero."

I leaned against one of the streetlamps, still catching my breath, staring at the skyline of the city. I was standing in the place where I'd taken her on our first date. She'd worn a dress that was too big, and her hair had stuck to our lips when we kissed.

"I miss you," I told her, wondering how many times in the upcoming months I would go out for this same jog, make this same phone call, and hear these same responses.

"I miss you," she whispered.

She was so quiet; I almost hadn't heard her.

I closed my eyes, waiting for the calm to come. "This is so fucking hard, Jess."

"Do you remember what you used to tell me when I was pregnant and miserable and cranky and hot? You'd tell me to take a deep breath and think about what it would be like once our baby was born. And how, after the delivery, those months of hell would be completely forgotten."

"I remember…"

I opened my lids and watched the college rowers practicing in the water in front of me and the cars speeding over the bridge to Cambridge and the joggers passing on the walkway behind me.

From here, I could see everything, and that was why Jesse loved it so much.

"I jogged to our spot."

"How's it look?"

I smiled. "The same."

"Now, how's the skyline going to look when it has an Emery Black design in the middle of it?"

I could see the space where the tower was going to be built. I could visualize how it would fit between the structures on both sides and how far it would reach in the sky.

My head shook in amazement. "I still can't believe it."

"Believe it. It's happening, and you're going to survive this. I promise."

Her voice turned quiet again, and I checked the screen to make sure we hadn't been disconnected. When I did, I saw the time. I'd been gone almost twenty minutes, and it would take that long to get home. It wouldn't matter how fast I went; we'd still be late in meeting the builder. But at least, if I headed to the brownstone now, rush hour would be over, and it wouldn't take us long to get to his office.

"Jesse, I'm going to run back. I love you."

Once I heard her say it back, I tucked my phone into my pocket, and I started my jog.

THIRTY-TWO
JESSE
BEFORE

"*AUTUMN MADE a promise to herself that day,*" my father read from the book he held in his hands. "*She would never, ever take anything for granted again.*" He shut the large hardcover and looked up, meeting my eyes.

I was sitting in a wingback chair across from him in his library while Tommy sat next to me. This was where my family spent every Sunday. Mom insisted on cooking, and Viv would hang out with her in the kitchen, helping her make dinner. Emery could be found on the couch, watching whatever New England game was on. Tommy would be with me and Dad in the library. I'd choose a book off one of the shelves, and my father would read to us. Sometimes, Tommy would play on his tablet, and other times, he'd work on art, but he was always listening. I knew a day would come when he wouldn't want to sit in here with his papa and me, and that was why I was soaking up every second of this.

"I've read that one at least four times," I said to Tommy about the book my dad had just closed.

I wouldn't classify it as young adult. There were scenes certainly inappropriate for him to hear, words too mature and unsuitable for young ears. But I didn't believe in sheltering my kids when it came to literature. It was art. I wanted them to experience things the way it had been intended.

"You read books more than once?" Tommy inquired.

I nodded. "If I enjoy it enough, I do."

"So do I," my father said, slowly pushing himself out of the chair and moving toward one of the rows. The book he grabbed was old and black and severely worn. I knew it well. He handed it to Tommy. "I've read this one almost forty times."

"Forty?" Tommy questioned.

"That's right," Dad replied. "My father gave it to me when I graduated high school. He died a few years later, and I started a tradition of reading it every year on his birthday. I've never missed a June."

"Wow," Tommy said, turning the novel over in his hands. "Maybe, one day, I'll read it."

He eventually gave the book back, and Dad returned it to the shelf and said, "How about you go check on Nana and your sister and see if they've made us something to snack on?"

My son's face lit up. "I'll be back in a minute."

Tommy rushed up from his chair, and I called out, "Please shut the door behind you. Thank you." I waited until he closed it before I turned to my father. "Are you okay?"

I didn't like the way he was looking at me.

"I want to talk to you ..." He went back to the same seat, sitting as slowly as he had stood. "Something's wrong."

"What is it, Dad?"

"I don't feel right."

I assessed him the same way I would do to one of my kids, looking for flushed cheeks and glossy eyes. Listening for a runny nose and a cough. I saw and heard nothing.

"Do you want to go to the hospital?" I asked.

He shook his head. "They won't be able to help me."

"Urgent care?"

"No, it's not like that." He paused, and my heart began to pound. "I need to start with my primary doctor, and I want you to come with me."

My parents had always been so healthy. The most serious diagnosis had only required an appendix removal, and that had happened before I was born. Neither of them even got sick in the winter with anything worse than a cold. That was why hearing him tell me he didn't feel right came as such a surprise.

"I'm sure this is all nothing," I told him. "When the seasons change, I always feel a little off myself. My allergies kick in, and I don't feel grounded. You might even want to wait a few weeks and see if it blows over. Then, we can always call the doctor and get you in."

In a tone I rarely heard from my father, he said, "You're not listening, Jesse. I'm telling you, something is wrong with me."

I felt the blood drain from my face. I felt the churning in my stomach. I felt the tremors shaking my entire body.

He would see none of that.

Instead, in the calmest voice, I told him, "I'll talk to Mom, and we'll call the doctor first thing in the morning."

When he exhaled, it almost sounded like a whistle. "I don't want Mom to know. That's why I'm coming to you."

"What?" My back went straight. "Why?"

He used the same voice again. "Because I don't."

He glanced away, telling me that was all I would be getting from him. If he wanted me to know more, he would have said it.

I didn't understand. My mother was always the first person he went to. Their marriage was strong. They were best friends. There was still so much love between them. She should have been in this chair, not me.

I didn't want to question him again and have him push me away, so if this was his wish, I would support it—for now. And, since Mom wasn't here to take the lead, I had to. "I'll call your doctor and get you an appointment for this week."

He didn't relax, but I saw relief now that he knew I would help.

"What about your work schedule?" he asked.

"I'll figure it out; don't worry."

I watched the rise and fall of his chest, the way his fingertips turned white as he pressed them against his thighs. Each breath almost seemed like a task for his body.

There were only two times in my life when I had been truly terrified, and both were when I'd birthed my children, waiting to hear their cries as the doctor held each one in his hands.

This was the third time.

As I looked in my father's eyes, I saw something that made me feel even worse.

He was as terrified as me.

THIRTY-THREE
CHARLOTTE

CHARLOTTE WAS IN THE KITCHEN, holding open the door to the fridge, when she heard Emery come home. She followed his sound, his steps getting louder until he walked into the kitchen. As she took in her boss post-run, she started to squeeze the cold metal door with both hands. He was dressed in a pair of gray sweatpants, a fleece jacket, and sneakers. He was sweaty, flushed, and devastatingly handsome.

But, as Charlotte watched him go over to the sink and gulp down a glass of water, she remembered how awkward things had been earlier this morning when she stared at him in the towel. She didn't want him to catch her gawking again, so she glanced back toward the fridge, pretending to search for something.

"I know we missed the meeting," Emery said from behind her, breaking a silence that had lasted far too long.

His tone didn't have the stress and anger from before, telling Charlotte the run had helped or maybe he'd had a conversation with Jesse and she had calmed him down. Either way, Emery wasn't the same person as when Charlotte had heard him on the phone.

Now, she hoped her news would make him feel even better.

"You didn't miss anything," she said, seeing a block of Havarti Marion must have picked up on her way here. "I rescheduled our meeting."

"To when?"

"Two," she said casually. "That was his only opening." She finally looked over her shoulder. "The inspection department called this morning and asked you in for an emergency meeting, and that's why you couldn't make it to him by nine."

"That meeting isn't until tomorrow."

"The builder doesn't know that."

A faint smile spread across his lips, and it pleased Charlotte so much to see it.

She grinned in response and glanced back at the fridge. "Hungry?" When she didn't get a reply, she added, "Since Marion is busy cleaning, I was going to make a sandwich, if you want one."

"It's ten in the morning."

She gazed over her shoulder once more and teased, "What, you can't have bread before noon?"

He laughed, and she loved that sound. "No, I can."

"Good. Then, I'll make us one that's more breakfast-y."

She filled her arms with ingredients and brought it over to the gas range. It took her several trips back to the fridge before everything was spread out and organized on the counter.

"Coffee or juice?" he asked.

She cracked two eggs into the fry pan. "I'll grab us drinks; don't worry."

He ignored her and went over to the coffeemaker, taking a mug out of the cabinet. "Do you want one?"

She nodded, only because he was making it.

"Do you put anything in yours?" he asked.

This was the first time Emery had waited on her, and she found it charming.

She pointed toward the refrigerator. "A heavy splash of the flavored creamer. That's it."

She reduced the heat on the eggs, put the bread into the toaster, and sliced the tomatoes to get them ready. Once the whites of the eggs were cooked, she began to layer the sandwich, finishing the large stack with a piece of smoked salmon. She added fresh fruit to the plates and brought them over to the table where Emery had the coffees, silverware, and napkins waiting.

She was just taking a seat when he said, "I didn't think to ask Adam if he wanted anything."

"I did," she replied. "He ate before he came over and isn't hungry. I also checked in with Luz to make sure everything was perfect back at home, and it is."

He shook his head as he put his napkin on his lap. "Thanks for handling it all."

She smiled and cut her sandwich in half, chewing slowly, letting all the different flavors settle on her tongue.

Emery kept his whole and bit off one of the corners. "*Mmm*," he said. Yolk dripped onto his plate, and he scooped it up by smearing the top of his sandwich into it. "When I saw you put on the cream cheese, I thought you were crazy."

Charlotte laughed behind her napkin to hide her mouthful. "I know it seems like an odd choice, but it complements the smoked salmon and tomato so well."

Several seconds passed before he said, "This is outstanding."

"If you like this one, wait until you try my grilled cheese with tomato soup."

The older Charlotte got, the more of a foodie she became, experimenting with the ingredients she could combine to create new tastes. She attributed that to a childhood full of mostly bland carbohydrates. It wasn't until college when she'd finally gotten to sample seafood and different cuts of meat. She hadn't stopped trying new foods ever since.

"I'd better keep up these runs, or you're going to put a good twenty on me."

Charlotte swallowed. "I can stop making the bread—"

"Please don't," he said, interrupting her. "I'm really enjoying it."

She warmed from his response but didn't show him that. Instead, she shifted in her seat, nervous to even bring up the conversation she had overheard today. But she had to. Her role was to support him; therefore, he needed to be honest with her.

"Emery, is there anything I can do to fix what happened between you and the builder?"

He took another bite. After freeing up his hands, he wrapped one around his mug. "His foreman is at the site, doing some measurements, and he thinks my numbers are going to be off when the ground thaws."

"And you say?"

"These designs took months' worth of research and calculations, hundreds of factors weighing in, including the change in temperature. For a foreman—not even an engineer or construction manager—to make such a prediction is ludicrous and far above his scope of knowledge."

Charlotte brought the coffee up to her mouth, taking several drinks from it, liking it even more because of who had made it. "Sounds like there's only one thing we can do."

"What's that?"

"Bring him your research and data and prove his ass wrong."

His smile grew to more than just a hint. Now, it covered the bottom half of his face and reached all the way to his eyes.

Charlotte already knew what he was going to say back to her, but hearing, "You're right," still made her whole morning, and so did the sight of his empty plate.

THIRTY-FOUR
JESSE
BEFORE

"SOMEONE'S BEEN BITTEN by the library bug," Bay joked when she joined me on the couch.

I closed the heavy paperback as I glanced up at her. "It feels better in here than it does out there," I admitted.

That wasn't entirely true, but it was close.

Life outside those double doors was extremely hard. The library was just simple, peaceful, and the air was filled with the aroma of books. After the morning I'd had at Cinched and the lunchtime visit I'd spent with Dad, I would be happy to stay in this spot for the rest of the night.

Bay crossed her legs, her hands resting on her knee. "I work here, and I would even agree with that statement."

Whenever Bay stopped to chat, we only ever talked about my dad and reading, never her. I'd completely monopolize every conversation.

"I'm terribly embarrassed right now," I said to her. "But I don't even know what you do here at the library."

"I'm the director of historical resources, which means I

focus on community outreach, fundraising, literacy programs, things like that."

"You're the face of the library."

She stopped to consider what I'd said. "I guess I am."

"Very impressive."

"Thank you." She smiled. "I don't get to hang out in the stacks as much as I'd like." She turned her head, checking the aisles on both sides of the sofa. "I miss it when I'm away for too long."

"Someone's been bitten by the bug, too."

"It's my happy place."

I wrapped my arm around the back of the couch and faced her a little more. "Same." I breathed in the scent. "It's heavenly." Wanting to keep the topic on her, I asked, "How was your week?"

Her face immediately lit up. "It's been a good one."

I knew that expression. Every woman did. It was the look that came across your face when you'd met a man you instantly connected with.

"He's definitely doing something right," I said.

Her cheeks turned pink. "I'm that obvious, huh?" She didn't wait for me to respond. "Things are new. Like, four-dates new."

I propped up my elbow and rested my face against my palm. "You're at that stage where everything makes you tingle."

She lowered her voice. "It feels like my skin is on fire."

I knew that feeling.

"What's he like?" I inquired.

"He's tall, semi-athletic, cute but not gorgeous, with the most contagious personality."

"He sounds perfect."

She pulled her hair onto one side, her fingers combing the long strands. "He kind of is."

"How did you meet?"

"He's the branch manager at my sister's bank. I went there to help straighten out her accounts, and he assisted us."

I quietly clapped my hands together. "Getting a non-customer's phone number before she leaves the branch? I'm impressed."

She chuckled. "Don't give him that much credit. I ran into him two weeks later at the grocery store, and that's where he asked me out."

"You know what? I like that even better," I thought out loud. I studied her for a few seconds. "I can see how much you like him."

"I do." She shrugged. "But it's so soon to really tell."

"When's the next date?"

"Tomorrow." She glanced down at her hand as she circled the thin silver band around her middle finger. "We saw each other last night, and he's already talking about plans for next week." When she looked up again, I saw her concern. "We're moving fast."

"No, you're not." I paused, collecting my thoughts. "I learned something when my dad got sick, something I wish I had known a long time ago." Her hand went to my shoulder, and her fingers were hugging me. "If the banker feels right, then let it happen. Just don't live with regret. You don't want to get to the end and wish you could have done it differently. You want to get there and think you lived one hell of a life."

I watched her soak in my words and process them.

And then she glanced at her watch and said, "This is going

to sound nuts, but I'm leaving here in fifteen minutes. Do you want to come with me and grab a drink?"

"I would love to."

"Great." She pushed herself to the edge of the couch. "I'm going to go take care of a few things, and I'll come get you when I'm done."

"Sounds good."

As she left, I reached into my purse to take out my phone. I never usually checked it while I was inside the library, but I felt it vibrating next to me on the couch. I scrolled through the notifications. There were over a hundred of them. One in particular made my eyes fill.

Dad: Hi, dollface.

"Oh no," Bay said as she rejoined me on the couch. "What happened while I was gone?"

With a wet tissue in my hand, I glanced up from the screen. I didn't know how many times I'd read those three words. I couldn't stop staring at them, visualizing the process he had gone through to type each letter.

All of that work ... for me.

I showed Bay my phone, so she knew what had made me so emotional.

"*Awww,*" she sighed. "He must be feeling better?"

I'd told her nothing about my dad's diagnosis or how he was sending me that message or how long it had taken him to get the letters on the screen. If I was going to have that conversation, I needed a drink.

"Let's go get a cocktail," I told her.

I got up from the couch, sticking my phone back in my bag

and hanging the long leather strap over my shoulder. With Luz scheduled to pick up Tommy from school and Viv at Trever's, I wouldn't have to look at the screen again.

"There's a place not far from campus that makes an incredible margarita," she said.

"No need to say any more. You had me at tequila."

THIRTY-FIVE
JESSE
AFTER

USING MY KEY, I went in through the back door of my parents' house. To me, it would always be called that, and at this time of the morning, Mom would be in the sunroom. That bright, airy space was her place, like the library was my father's.

After making a turn at the powder room, I reached the double doors I knew so well and paused in front of them. I did that every time I came here, wanting so desperately to go inside and run my fingers across the spines of the books and have my eyes fall onto the titles.

I couldn't.

Neither could Mom, which was why she kept the doors closed.

I forced my feet to continue moving, going deeper in their house until I reached the sunroom. Mom sat in a white wicker chair, her body facing the large windows. There was a crossword puzzle on her lap, a pen, and a pair of reading glasses.

"Hi," I said as I walked over to her.

Slowly, she turned and looked at me. "Hi, pumpkin."

I remembered a time when she'd had an entirely different voice. Happy, cheerful, full of energy and charisma. Now, it was just like my smile ... faded.

As I bent down to give her a kiss, she put her hand on my face. I stopped, not going any closer, and she said, "I just want to look at you."

With my mask on so incredibly tight, I clung my fingers around hers, squeezing so hard that both of our hands were shaking. My heart contracted, and a boulder moved into the back of my throat.

I wasn't going to cry. I couldn't do that to her.

She needed my strength, not my weakness.

"You look beautiful," she said as she stared at me.

Oh, Mom.

I pulled her hand off my cheek, kissing the back of it, breathing in her vanilla scent before I took a seat in the next chair.

My parents had a meadow behind their house where you could see the first hints of spring, and it was just starting to come through now. The snow had finally cleared from the ground, and the air wasn't as brisk. Rising from the grass were tiny buds of wildflowers that would be gorgeous once they bloomed.

I wished my father could see this.

I wanted just one more spring with him.

"What are you up to today?" she asked.

I crossed my legs and glanced toward her. "I'm going to go to the library, pick up Tommy from school, have dinner with the kids and Emery. Why don't you come over? Luz is making her famous pork enchiladas. Charlotte brought us some lavender and poppy seed bread that we'll have for dessert."

"Sounds wonderful."

We still spent Sundays together as a family, and she was invited to our home every night for dinner and on the evenings we went out to eat, too. Unfortunately, I could only get her to commit once or twice a week, if I was lucky.

"I made her mandarin banana bread this morning when I woke up," she said. "Don't forget to take a piece when you leave. It's delicious."

I smiled; she just didn't see me.

My mom had met Charlotte by the second week of her employment. Since they both enjoyed spending so much time in the kitchen, they had a lot in common, and I often found them chatting.

"It smelled so good when I came in," I lied.

The only thing I ever smelled in this house was my father. His scent was everywhere.

"I've been thinking about Cinched," she said.

I shook my head and then glanced toward her. "Oh, yeah?"

"Are you going to go back to work?"

It didn't matter what answer I gave her. But I went with the truth and said, "No." I had a feeling that wouldn't satisfy her, so I added, "I'm really enjoying being home with the kids."

"I was hoping you would say that." I loved hearing the warmth in her voice even if it wasn't the same temperature it had been before. "One day, it's just going to be you and Emery in that house. You'll no longer be finding your daughter's clothes on the floor or begging your son to put away his tablet. There won't be any laughter coming from the bedrooms upstairs. Dinners will be for two instead of four."

My hands were in my lap, hidden, clenched together like my throat.

"Those are the years when you're going to miss the noise, so enjoy every second of it, kiddo ..." She took a breath, and her lips quivered. "Because the silence is practically torture."

I wanted to rest my hand on top of hers, but I couldn't move.

I wanted to respond.

I couldn't do that either.

So, I stayed facing the meadow, just like my mother did on the other side of me, and I tried not to have a panic attack in her sunroom. It was leading to that, and I'd have to excuse myself soon, locking the bathroom door behind me while I unraveled. Once it was over, when I was able to control at least half of what was happening in me, I would put my mask back on and rejoin my mom.

She would think I was sad.

And I was.

Oh God.

We were two women broken from the inside out.

But for entirely different reasons.

THIRTY-SIX
JESSE
BEFORE

"AMYOTROPHIC LATERAL SCLEROSIS," my father's doctor said.

I was sitting on the other side of his desk in the chair farthest from him. It didn't matter how far away I was. It was so loud in my head; it was as though he were holding a megaphone, speaking directly into my ear.

Each word was like a fucking bomb.

My feet bounced from the aftershock. I wobbled in my chair. My body shook.

If there were a bucket in front of me, I was sure I would throw up into it.

The doctor's lips were still moving. I heard nothing else that he said.

I could only focus on one thing.

The diagnosis.

ALS.

I had known it in my gut before the testing even started.

I had known it was going to lead to this moment.

But, now, I was here.
And …
Oh God.
I … grabbed fingers.
And I squeezed them with the little strength I had left.

THIRTY-SEVEN
CHARLOTTE

"ANYONE NEED A REFILL?" Charlotte heard Jesse say from the living room where she was having wine with some friends.

Charlotte was in the kitchen, making several sandwiches. This was the first time she'd left the office all day, only having time to inhale a few granola bars that she kept at her desk. Work was just too busy to take a break.

Construction had started on 3 Stuart Street, and if she'd thought she had a lot to do before they broke ground, it didn't even compare to the workload she had now.

Charlotte looked up just as Jesse walked in.

"Hi," Jesse said. "I didn't even hear you come down."

Charlotte smiled and finished spreading the apricot jam over the slices of ham. "I tried to be quiet. I didn't want to interrupt you and your friends."

Jesse returned the smile and moved over to the island. "Looks delicious."

"Do you want one? I can grab two more pieces of bread. It won't be a problem."

"That's kind of you to offer, but I've been snacking in there." She used her head to point to the living room. "Thank you for making one for Emery and the kids."

Luz had only been able to work a few hours, getting things ready for Jesse's girls' night, but she wasn't able to make dinner. When Charlotte had arrived this morning, Jesse had come into the office and asked if she wouldn't mind filling in. Because Charlotte had been so engrossed all day, she didn't have time to make anything more than sandwiches.

"Happy to do it," Charlotte said, layering in some pickled onion before she put on the top slice.

While Jesse went to the other side of the kitchen, Charlotte wrapped up the sandwiches for Tommy and Viv and put those in the fridge for them to eat when they returned home.

She was just adding some potato salad to both plates when she heard Jesse shout, "Damn it!"

Charlotte turned just in time to see the bottle of wine that she had been trying to open go flying around the corner of the counter and crash on the floor.

"Shit!" Jesse snapped when the glass shattered, and dark red liquor splashed everywhere.

"Let me help." Charlotte rushed over, immediately bending to the floor. "I'll get the glass. I don't want you to cut yourself." She began to pick up the bigger pieces.

"I'll ... get the paper towels," Jesse replied.

While Charlotte filled her palm with glass, Jesse slowly wiped the cabinets where it had splattered and the large puddles on the floor.

Once the larger pieces were picked up, Charlotte swept

the rest into a dustpan and said, "Looks like it's all clean," after doing a quick scan to make sure she'd gotten it all.

"Thank you." Jesse stood next to her. "I really appreciate your help."

"It's my pleasure."

Charlotte went back to the counter, putting the rest of the potato salad on the plates. As she turned around, she saw Jesse with the wine opener back in her hand, and it looked like she was having a hard time getting the cork out.

"You know, when I was in college, I won a contest for being the fastest corker in my sorority," Charlotte said. "Allow me?"

Jesse chuckled. "Oh, I have to see this."

Charlotte stepped in, twisting the metal deeper into the cork before she began the process of pulling it out.

"Join us," Jesse said, catching Charlotte off guard. "Just for one drink. As a way to thank you for all your help tonight." When Charlotte didn't say anything, Jesse went on, "You and Emery have been working so hard, and I'm sure you have a long night ahead of you. Unplugging for a few minutes might help." When Charlotte still didn't answer, Jesse took her phone out of her back pocket, hit the screen, and held it up to her ear. "Baby, I'm stealing Charlotte for a second to have a drink with the girls. She'll bring your dinner up in fifteen. Love you." Jesse hung up, not giving Emery a chance to respond, and then she stuck both plates in the fridge. She turned toward Charlotte when she said, "Come on."

Charlotte was relieved she hadn't had to say anything or give Jesse an answer or discuss this with Emery. Even though one of her responsibilities was to make sure his wife and the kids were taken care of, Charlotte didn't think this was what Emery had had in mind when he assigned her that task.

"A super-quick drink," Charlotte agreed to while Jesse put the bottle of wine under her arm, and she followed Jesse into the living room.

"Ladies," Jesse said as she stood in front of the couch, "meet Charlotte. Charlotte, that's Alicia, Karen, Jamie, and Belle."

Each of the women smiled after their name was said.

"Hi, everyone." Charlotte waved as she looked at their faces, appreciating the generous welcome.

"Emery has kept Charlotte trapped in the office all day, and I say she needs a little wine and girl time before she goes back to work."

"We're happy to have you join our party," Alicia said.

"Let's get you a glass," Belle stated, grabbing one from the table Luz had set up that held the trays of appetizers. Belle then took the bottle from Jesse and poured Charlotte a glass.

Charlotte took it into her hand and held it into the air. "Cheers, girls." The heavy cabernet warmed her throat as she swallowed.

"The cranberry bread you've been snacking on tonight was made by Charlotte," Jesse told the group.

"You have to give me the recipe," Karen said to Charlotte. "Cranberry is my husband's favorite. He will die if he tries this bread."

"I'm happy to pass it along," Charlotte replied, taking the end seat on the couch next to Jesse. "It's also really good if you add in a touch of almond. I can give you that recipe, too, if you'd like."

"I would love that," Karen responded.

"How are things going in Boston?" Alicia asked.

Charlotte took another small sip. "The building is going to be spectacular. We're just anxious to see it all come together."

"Dennis and I are interested in one of the condos," Alicia said.

"In Emery's building?" Jesse inquired, her face beaming.

"For the last year, we've been going back and forth about having a weekend home," Alicia explained to all the women. "We love the city, and we think it would be such an honor to live in a home our best friend designed."

"Oh, Alicia," Jesse said, her hand going to her heart. "Emery is going to be over the moon when he hears this."

"That's if we can even get a unit," Alicia said. "According to the news, it's forecasted to be the fastest-selling building in Boston's history."

"I'll do everything I can to help," Charlotte said to Alicia, feeling all the other women staring at her. "I work closely with the sales office, which will be launching in a few months. When you're ready, I can give them your information, so you're contacted when the units are released."

Alicia smiled at her and said, "You're a doll."

Charlotte gave her a grin in return, and the topic shifted to a television show. Charlotte didn't want to rush out, but she was starving, and she was sure Emery was, too, while both sandwiches were hardening in the fridge.

"Help yourself to a refill," Jesse said, looking at Charlotte's almost-empty glass.

"Thank you," Charlotte replied. "But I think I've reached my fill."

"I get it. When work calls, it's the only thing on your mind."

Charlotte nodded and stood from the couch. "Thanks for the drink, ladies." She waved to each of them.

"Thanks for joining us," one of them said as Charlotte made her way back to the kitchen.

While she was grabbing the sandwiches out of the fridge, she could still hear the women chatting. And, even though she tried not to listen, she couldn't help it once she heard her name.

"Charlotte's gorgeous," one of them said.

"And so helpful."

"With quite the body on her."

"Listen, if my husband brought home an assistant who looked like Charlotte, I'd be hiring myself a personal trainer, getting the fillers I'd been putting off, and talking to my gyno about some type of rejuvenation."

Charlotte heard a few of the women laugh and was holding her breath as she waited for Jesse to respond.

"Don't be silly," Jesse finally said. "Charlotte is the best thing that's ever happened to Emery's business. She's lovely, as you all just witnessed ..."

Charlotte stood with her back to the wall, both plates in her hands, anxious about what was going to be said next.

"And, honey, I already get the fillers."

Charlotte felt herself relax, and she walked upstairs with a smile on her face.

THIRTY-EIGHT
JESSE
BEFORE

WHEN I WALKED into the library, my father didn't glance up from his book. His eyes stayed focused on the large hardcover in his lap as he completely ignored the sound of the door closing and my heels clicking on the hardwood floor.

Even when I bent down and kissed his cheek and said, "Hi, Daddy," I wasn't acknowledged.

My father was on the quieter side, the shyer of my two parents. When it came to our relationship, he wasn't overly talkative, but he wasn't speechless either.

His silence told me something was wrong.

I sat in the chair next to his, my body facing him. "Dad, please talk to me."

Several seconds passed before he responded, "I have nothing to say."

He was angry because I had told my mother about the two doctor's appointments I had gone to with him and the first round of tests that had been done. He hadn't told her, and someone needed to, so I had taken it upon myself. I would always be there for him, but my mother needed to be there, too. She had been devastated to be hearing it from me, petrified of what the results would be, and confused as to why he hadn't told her.

My mother had confronted him two days ago, and my father hadn't spoken to me since.

"I don't understand, Dad."

When he looked up, I almost gasped from the pain in his eyes.

"You're young, healthy. You don't lie in bed, thinking about how you're losing control of your body, feeling weak, and unbalanced. I can't even open a goddamn pickle jar anymore." Frustration poured through his voice. "Thank God you don't know what it feels like. But, until you do, you can't sit there and tell me what I should and shouldn't do."

He was nervous; I could understand why. When we'd gone to his primary doctor, he'd referred us to a neurologist, who we'd met with last week. During that meeting, my father's symptoms were discussed in much greater detail, and a physical exam was performed, assessing Dad's reflexes and movement—things I hadn't known were even a problem. The doctor told us there could be many different things going on that would cause these symptoms. Muscular diseases were much harder to diagnose because many of them didn't have tests; they just had to rule things out. The first step was taking his blood and urine, which was done last week along with an MRI. Those results had already come in, and more testing had been set up.

What was missing from all of this was my mother.

"Dad, Mom should have been there, and she needs to be there, going forward."

He turned his head away, refusing to look at me. "That's your opinion. Ultimately, this was my decision, and you took that away from me."

I tried to keep my voice down. Mom was out, walking, but could return any minute, and I wouldn't hear her if she was outside the door. "What is going on? Why don't you want her there?"

"If it were up to me, I wouldn't tell her at all."

Shock blasted through my body. I couldn't believe what I was hearing. Or how to process this. Or how someone I loved could be this selfish.

I got up and sat on the small table in front of his chair, getting myself as close to him as I could. "Why, Daddy? Make me understand this."

"I don't want her to worry about me." He was biting back so much emotion, and the sight made my own chin quiver. "Once she knows there's something wrong, she'll be watching me like a goddamn hawk. I'll become a burden, and I don't want that. I just want to be the man she married."

He clasped his hand and hissed from the pain.

I did everything I could to keep the tears in when I said, "A burden?" I shook my head to regain my composure. "You're her husband. You're not a burden to anyone."

"I will be."

He thought he had the disease that had been mentioned at the end of the exam, and when I'd gone home that night, I'd researched everything I could on it. The symptoms my dad had mentioned were listed.

Every single one of them.

It didn't mean anything.

Or it could mean everything.

But, if my father had ALS, the disease the doctor had said last because it was the worst-case scenario, then all of our lives were about to drastically change.

"We don't know anything yet," I reminded him. "Let's stay positive. The MRI—"

"Told us nothing. How sad that I was praying for it to show a tumor, which would explain why all of this is happening to me. But I don't have cancer. I have something worse. Something that can't be cured."

"Don't say that. There're lots of other things this could be—"

He clenched the armrests. "We both know what it is, Jesse. The tests are going to confirm it, and then I'll have three to five years before I'm on a ventilator."

I couldn't handle the thought of that or the image I saw in my head of my father with a tube down his throat in a hospital bed.

"Dad..."

His stare intensified. "The other reason I didn't want to tell your mother is because I don't want her looking at me with pity in her eyes. Pity makes me feel like I'm failing. I already feel enough of that."

My father had so much pride. He wasn't vulnerable or weak, and I could tell he felt both right now. It made me want to break for him.

"No one in this family would do that."

His face softened for just a second, and I saw a completely different side of his expression. It was as though he were letting me in, revealing how he was really feeling deep inside.

And what he showed me was ...

Terror.

And then it was gone, replaced with a cold, angry stare when he said, "Jesse ... it's the way you're looking at me right now."

THIRTY-NINE
CHARLOTTE

EMERY AND CHARLOTTE were in the backseat of an SUV, driving to his house after having just flown in from Boston where they'd spent the last three nights. Their time there had been busy, the days spent at the jobsite or at the builder's office. On occasion, they'd work at Emery's townhouse, but that was becoming less and less now that they were getting deeper into the construction.

The nights Charlotte stayed in Burlington were silent, the Boston ones so loud. She liked the mix, but she liked the noisy ones more. She enjoyed lying in bed at the hotel that was only a few blocks from Emery's place, wondering what he was doing, thinking of the small white towel he had been wrapped in. What he would look like if he were stretched out on his bed, wearing only that narrow piece of white fabric.

Those were the images Charlotte thought of when she touched herself.

Her skin heated as she glanced in his direction. He was so focused on the phone in his hand, his long, thin fingers tapping the screen. Charlotte couldn't stop her mind from wandering, thinking how those fingers would feel on her body. Her gaze moved up a few inches, remembering the dips of his chest and the definition in his shoulders. She lifted her stare once more and thought of the short hairs of his trimmed beard.

The urge to touch it was so strong; she had to turn away from him and face the window, concentrating on a view that didn't have him in it.

They were getting closer to his house, and the mountains were becoming more descriptive. The colors deepened. The edges of the cliffs grew sharper as they came into focus.

Charlotte looked up ahead, seeing the storefronts and homes and motorcycles. There was even a biker about a football field away, hugging the shoulder of the road. Charlotte recognized the bright blue base of the bicycle as one she'd seen in Emery's garage.

Once she studied the back of the woman who was riding it, she pointed out the window and said, "I think that's Jesse."

Emery immediately glanced up from his phone, and Charlotte watched his face. As he realized the woman was his wife, a smile sparked in his eyes. It quickly moved down his cheeks and to his mouth.

"That's her," he said.

He didn't use her name. He gave no details that described her, nothing endearing or memorable. But it was the sound of his voice and the look in his eyes that said it all.

Charlotte hoped, one day, a man would gaze at her the same way he was staring at Jesse.

And, if that person were Emery, that would be even better.

FORTY
JESSE
BEFORE

"IT'S time to discuss your options," my father's doctor said. He paused, waiting for an acknowledgment before saying any more.

As the seconds ticked by, I heard his cuff links scrape over his desk. Every roll of his thumbs caused the metal to drag across the wood again, and he repeated the action over and over.

All I wanted was silence, the sounds making this situation even more real.

Real was terrifying.

Unimaginable.

Unfathomable.

"Jesse ..."

I gasped.

It was as though he had snuck up behind me and shouted, *Boo*, in my ear. I'd expected to hear my name, but that didn't make it any less shocking.

It hurt.

Everything fucking hurt.

I couldn't move.

I couldn't speak.

All I could do was stare at him from the other side of the desk, listening to the *whoosh* of the metal, remembering when he had last said, "It's time to discuss your options."

My eyes shifted to his monitor. It showed all the tests that had been run—blood work, MRIs, muscle biopsies, an electromyography, nerve conduction studies. There had been so many, and they had taken months.

Months of questions.

Tears.

Needles and pain and stark white rooms and the smell of antibacterial and alcohol.

Oh God.

My eyes slowly lifted to the top of the screen where the name and diagnosis were listed. I had done that so many times in the past, seeing my dad's information there.

This time, it wasn't his.

It was mine.

Patient: Black, Jesse, 42
Diagnosis: Familial Amyotrophic Lateral Sclerosis (FALS)

One week ago, I'd sat in this same seat as my father's doctor read me my life sentence. My disease was different than my dad's. Where his was sporadic, mine was inherited, which made it more aggressive and one of the reasons I'd started showing symptoms at such a young age.

Two years.

That was how long the doctor had given me.

Twenty-four months, and I would never see my children or my husband again.

What am I supposed to do with this news? How am I supposed to live the rest of my time when I can feel myself dying? What if I pass this on to my children, whose chance of inheriting it is extremely high?

I swallowed, feeling the spit burn all the way down, before my stare moved back to the doctor's. "Yes," I whispered.

"There's a cocktail of medications I would like to start you on. One is designed to slow the atrophy, and the other is …"

I stopped listening. I already knew the drugs that were available, their side effects, how much insurance would cover. I knew an antidepressant would be added into the cocktail. I knew therapy for Emery, the kids, and me would be recommended. They were all going to need counseling while they watched me die.

I knew because I was living it right now.

Every week, I helped Mom arrange my father's pills. I paid whatever the insurance didn't cover for him. I attended the weekly sessions with the family therapist.

It was a nightmare.

For all of us.

Oh God.

I couldn't put them through it … again.

I couldn't make them hurt even worse. I couldn't make them terrified of a future without me because, once they found out, they would stop living.

And I needed them to live if I was going to die.

That was the reason I was taking this journey alone.

A week after being diagnosed, I returned here to discuss

my future. Except he didn't have to tell me. I saw it every time I looked at my father.

One day, I wouldn't be able to hide it from my family.

Right now, I still could.

"Tell me about death with dignity," I said.

My father had never asked the doctor that question. He hadn't considered it an option. I honestly believed that was because he hadn't known how bad it would get.

But my disease looked me straight in the eyes, and it showed me the torture it was going to put me through.

That was why I needed to know everything that was available to me.

There were several more swipes of his cuff links across the desk and a large inhale. "Act thirty-nine provides an end-of-life option when a patient has a life expectancy of six months or less."

My face was so numb that I didn't feel my lips part or, "Do I qualify?" come out of them.

His hands stopped moving, and suddenly, there was silence.

This was what I'd wanted all along.

Now that it was here, I couldn't stand it. It made every joint, every bone, every muscle ache even more.

"It's something we would discuss in great length."

"Dr. Moore …" I took a breath. It felt like his hands were around my throat, and he was squeezing, pressing his thumbs against my tongue, so it was almost impossible to speak. "Would I qualify?"

With every beat that passed, it was as though he were clenching me even tighter.

"When I determine your disease has progressed enough

where your life expectancy is six months or less, then yes, you would qualify."

He was willing to write the prescription. That was going to be my next question.

For the last week, I'd spent all my time at the library, researching Act 39, reading every article that had been written about the law. I learned the process, requirements, the steps the physician had to follow.

There was one major problem with the law.

The tremors weren't just in my hands now. They were going through my whole body, as high as my lips and as low as my toes.

I clung to my knees, holding them with all my strength when I said, "At the six-month mark, I'll be fully paralyzed with a feeding tube. More than likely, a ventilator."

Those words were so familiar.

I just never thought I'd use them to describe myself.

"Due to the way the law was written, it does mean you'll be between the middle and late stage." He paused. "However, the dose must be self-administered, so your hands can't be paralyzed."

By then, I would still be in a wheelchair with the start of slurred speech. Swallowing would begin to get challenging; large bites would choke me. Eventually, I'd lose the ability to speak.

It didn't matter how hard I tried to stop it or what medications I took.

If I cried.

Begged.

Prayed.

No one could save me.

At this point, not even God.

I tried to hide the emotion in my voice the same way I'd been masking my symptoms. "What if I want to die with dignity, Dr. Moore? Before I require a wheelchair and twenty-four-hour care? Before my family has to watch me disintegrate like my father?"

His expression never softened in my presence, not in all the years I'd been coming here and seeing him in the hospital, listening to him deliver more heartbreaking news. The man always stayed detached, and I was fine with that. I didn't come for his bedside manner. I came because he was the best. But, suddenly, there was a crack. A hint of emotion. And I felt it blast through me like a tremor so strong that it made me lose my balance.

Except, this time, I was sitting.

This time ... there was nowhere for me to fall.

"The law isn't negotiable, I'm afraid," he said.

And then it was gone, and aloofness was in its wake.

My throat closed.

All the air left my lungs.

Bile swirled in my stomach, and I knew I would throw it up the second I walked out of his office.

I'd completely lost control. I just wanted a little of it back, and he couldn't even give that to me.

This conversation wasn't about options.

It was about death.

"As your disease advances, we'll be seeing each other monthly, as you know. It's something we can talk about again in the future. In the meantime, let's discuss the medications I would like you to start ..."

I clenched my hands together the same way I had done

when he read me my diagnosis. I only had myself to hold on to. And, while I stared straight ahead, I watched a thick black line form at the top of my vision and travel to the floor.

My life was now divided.

There was the Jesse before her diagnosis and the Jesse after.

And both of us only had two years to live.

FORTY-ONE
JESSE
BEFORE

BAY'S EYES began to fill, her lips on the verge of quivering. "Jesse ..."

"Please don't look at me that way," I whispered.

Her sadness shifted to bewilderment while her fingers gripped my hand. "How am I looking at you?"

"With pity in your eyes," I told her.

My father had called me out for the same thing, and I hadn't realized I'd been doing it.

I was sure Bay hadn't either, so before she responded, I added, "What I need is someone I can get angry with, someone who will scream at my disease with me because, pretty soon ... I won't be able to."

She squeezed harder. "That's me."

In the year and a half I'd been coming here, this wasn't the first time I'd clung to her fingers. It wasn't the second or third either. I made sure she was working every time I came here, and with each conversation, I let her in a little further. Eventually, those talks had led to a friendship.

One that meant a great deal to me.

"I'm here, Jesse." Her face hardened just like I needed it to. "I'm going to be by your side while you fight this. You just tell me if you need anything."

I wasn't going to cry. I'd done enough of that.

Instead, I reached into my purse and pulled out the teal hardcover I'd finished this morning. It was the book with the gold lettering on the spine and flowers etched into the binding. I'd been thinking about it since I got diagnosed and checked it out again a few days ago.

I handed her the novel and said, "I want you to read this."

Her stare roamed over the title and the design on the front, how the flowers traveled across the spine and onto the back. "I remember when we talked about this book."

I'd forgotten to give her the title, so she could look it up. Then, life had happened, the days had slipped away, and it had no longer been important.

But, suddenly, it was.

Because ... I was out of time.

If I wanted something, I had to make it happen now.

"Please start it as soon as you can," I said softly.

"Tonight," she promised, and she dropped the book onto her lap. "Jesse, I have to ask you something." Her expression weakened but not enough to hurt. "I get why you haven't told your mom and your kids about your disease, but why haven't you said anything to Emery? You guys are so close; I figured he would be the first person you'd tell."

I tried to come up with an answer. I'd been trying to do that since Dr. Moore gave me the news. It would at least lessen the guilt I felt every time I looked at my husband, every time I told him I loved him. I'd even tried forcing myself to tell him the truth.

I just couldn't.

And then I remembered how my father hadn't wanted to tell my mother when he was going through the testing. When I'd asked him why, he couldn't explain his reasoning. If I hadn't been the one to share the news with her, I wasn't sure if he ever would have.

Now, I felt the same way about Emery.

He was my soul mate. My best friend. The only man I ever wanted to be with. There was no doubt in my mind he was perfect for me.

So, why couldn't I tell him I was dying?

I didn't have an explanation for that.

I just knew I wanted to protect him until I couldn't anymore. I wanted to keep all of his pain and hold it for myself.

Since there was no way I could describe that to her, not in a way she would understand, I pointed at the hardcover in her lap.

Rather than give her the answers, I was going to show her what they looked like. "Trust me when I say … read the book."

Birdie and I were in bed, the teal book with the gold flowers resting across my stomach.

While Bay had been reading it, I'd decided to buy my own copy, and tonight, the two of us had discussed the plot. With the kids at my mom's and Emery in New York City for work, I had the whole evening to spend with her at a restaurant, and we used up every minute of it.

The story had given Bay some clarity into my world. We broke down every level, every stage I would go through, and what that would look like. And, once she had a clearer picture of my future, I told her what I wanted from her.

Bay had changed my life from the moment we met. I'd told her that this evening and again when I hugged her good-bye. I wasn't the same person I had been before I went into the library today. I'd walked out, feeling so different, like the hands that had been choking me since my diagnosis were now squeezing just a little lighter.

It was that feeling, that tiny sense of relief, that caused me to pick up my phone and log into the medical portal of Dr. Moore's office. From there, I opened the tab that contacted the doctor, and I typed him a note.

Dr. Moore,
During one of my appointments, you mentioned something about a clinical trial that's starting for FALS patients. I would like to enroll immediately. Please have your receptionist call me, so I can schedule a time to come in.
I'm feeling extremely hopeful about this.
—Jesse Black

I set the phone on my nightstand and pulled the blanket up to my neck. Birdie was resting horizontally across Emery's empty side, her head inches from my pillow. She made a noise, and I turned toward her. All she wanted was my attention. She now had it. My heavy hand dropped onto her back, and as I moved it toward her face, I scratched each spot I passed.

It didn't matter if I had been hit with a tremor, if my hand shook, or if my arm felt too weak to hold up; Birdie didn't call me out on any of it. With her, I didn't have to wear a mask. I could tell her all the things I was scared of. The things I didn't tell Bay because a person could only handle so much, and I'd given her enough.

As though Birdie felt my relief tonight, she leaned forward and licked across my lips.

"Somehow," I told her, "it's going to be all right."

My dog knew something was happening inside of me. She had known the minute I did, when the symptoms were more than just sympathy shakes I felt every time I left my father. Now, whenever I was home, she wouldn't leave my side.

She put her face in front of mine and rested it there. Every few breaths, she'd touch her nose to my cheek. It was cold, wet, leaving a dampness behind.

I moved my fingers right behind her ears, rubbing her favorite spot. "I'm not going to tell them, Birdie."

It was all I'd thought about since I was diagnosed. Dad wasn't going to make it much longer. My family was already practically living at the hospital. The sadness between all of us was already far too thick.

I couldn't destroy them. Not again. Not like this and not this soon.

So, I refused to do it.

Birdie rubbed her nose around my cheek, smelling, licking the small tear at the corner of my eye.

"I know it's wrong," I told her. "I know I shouldn't hide this from them, but I have to."

When I took a breath, my throat tightened. It wasn't just from emotion. This was the new normal. Pain shot through the middle of my chest. It was as sharp as the blade of a machete, slicing me right in half. I wasn't going to survive this, but I would do what I needed to do for them.

The Before Jesse wouldn't have understood this, but the After admitted the hardest thing I had ever said, "Because I won't be their burden."

FORTY-TWO
CHARLOTTE

CHARLOTTE WAS SITTING at her desk in Emery's office, neck deep in soil reports for a house he was designing in Cape Cod, when she heard a knock. The door was open, and so were all the windows, the papers rustling from the cross-office breeze. When she heard the noise again, she realized it wasn't coming from outside, and she looked up. Her eyes immediately locked with Jesse's.

"Do you have a minute?"

"Sorry about that," Charlotte said. "Yes, of course. Please come in." She watched Jesse walk across the room and take a seat on the couch in front of her desk.

"I was hoping we could get everything finalized for Viv's graduation party along with the details of our trip."

Charlotte pulled out the notebook she reserved just for Jesse—responsibilities she'd inherited now that she had several months of employment under her belt. She then grabbed a pen and began to read her notes out loud, "Starting with the party, it looks like the mock-ups the florist designed were approved, and their invoice has been paid in full. They'll be here five hours before to set up." Charlotte attached the most recent photos the florist had sent to a text message and forwarded it to Jesse. When she saw Jesse look at her phone, she added, "I made sure each of your changes were implemented before I gave them the final okay."

Jesse swiped her finger over the screen, finally glancing up several seconds later. "They look great."

Charlotte marked that line and moved on to the next item. "The caterer was waiting for the final head count, which I gave to him two days ago. There will be food stations set up outside—one in the kitchen and another in the living room. There will also be three bars—two bartenders behind each one. The final tasting is a week from Tuesday, and he'll be bringing everything here." Charlotte went to the bottom of the page, seeing the only thing that was left. "I ordered the whoopie pie cake along with the mini whoopie pies in all the different flavors, including three vegan options, and it will be delivered the morning of."

"Viv is going to be so thrilled."

Her voice was so quiet; the sound of it caused Charlotte to glance up.

As a mom, it had to be extremely difficult to watch your firstborn prepare to go off to college. Charlotte wouldn't know; she still didn't even own a plant. But she imagined the challenges a mother would face in that circumstance and how emotional it could be.

And that seemed to be where Jesse was—that emotional place.

Since they had covered all of her notes, Charlotte changed the subject to one she hoped would be a little happier. "Emery said he'd discussed the trip with you, and you're still undecided on where you would like to go."

According to Emery, the family took a two-week vacation every July. They had traveled all over the world, places as extravagant as Dubai and as remote as a safari in Africa. The kids and Emery would make their suggestions, but ultimately, the location was up to Jesse. She always made the arrangements and surprised them after it was booked.

Jesse had her own notebook, which she was writing notes in as Charlotte read off all the updates. But, once Charlotte shifted conversations, Jesse had shut it and was now holding it against her chest. It almost looked like she was hugging it.

"He's pushing for Alaska," she said.

Charlotte had never been, but she knew people who had gone, and she'd seen pictures and videos from their trips. She also knew how badly Emery wanted to go and how many times he had brought it up to her. Since it didn't seem like Jesse's mind was made up, Charlotte felt obligated to try to persuade her.

"Alaska is absolutely gorgeous," she said. "The mountains and wildlife, the peacefulness." She crossed her legs, getting more comfortable in the chair. "I could look into weeklong cruises, maybe one out of Seattle—"

"No." When Jesse realized how loud she'd spoken, she shook her head and found that gentle tone again. "Boston is where I want to go."

Out of all the places they still hadn't traveled to, Charlotte was surprised Jesse had chosen the spot she visited the most, where Viv would be moving to in a few months. But Emery had told Charlotte his wife had a deep love for that city; it was where they had first met, and she tried to go as often as she could.

As Charlotte looked at her, she could see that love. "What day would you like to fly in with the kids?"

"Friday. We'll stay through the following weekend and fly back to Vermont on Sunday."

Charlotte looked at her calendar, mapping the logistics of Jesse's request, factoring in the time she and Emery were scheduled to be in Boston. "It looks like you'll be meeting Emery there." She gazed up at his wife to make sure this was all right with her.

"That's fine."

Charlotte wrote as she spoke, "I'll coordinate the plane to pick you and the kids up and take you into Boston whatever time you'd like." Charlotte paused to scroll to the next month just to confirm. "Unfortunately, your return flight will also be without Emery since we're scheduled to be in Boston at the beginning of that week."

"Not a problem." She pushed herself off the couch. "Thanks for your help, Charlotte." She waved, and just as she took a step, her foot wobbled. Her other foot didn't help steady her at all, and she fell onto the ground.

"Jesse ..." Charlotte gasped, standing from her chair, rushing over to her.

Charlotte got halfway there before Jesse's hand went into the air, signaling for Charlotte to stop. Charlotte did, staying perfectly still right where she was, and she watched Jesse catch her breath.

Not a single word was said between the two women.

Eventually, Jesse put her palms on the floor and pushed herself up. "I didn't eat breakfast." She sighed, her voice as soft as it had been before. "And then I biked six miles, and I just forgot to eat when I got home."

Jesse's face was flushed, and her hands were shaking; Charlotte noticed both. But, before Charlotte could respond, her phone vibrated in her pocket, and she took it out to look at the screen.

It was an e-mail from Emery.

A warmth spread through Charlotte as she thought of her boss, and that was quickly followed by a long stretch of guilt that burrowed into her chest, eating a hole straight through to her heart.

She got the same feeling every time she was in Jesse's presence.

She hated it. More than anything.

But that didn't stop her from thinking about Jesse's husband—even if she found that thought extremely overwhelming.

Charlotte put the phone back in her pocket and said, "How about I make you a caprese sandwich? Luz picked up some fresh tomatoes this morning from the farmers market, and they'll taste delicious between a baguette with some fresh basil and mozzarella."

Jesse had been fixing her clothes as Charlotte was speaking, but she stopped and turned toward Charlotte. Charlotte was surprised to see there were tears in Jesse's eyes, and her lips were trembling.

Suddenly, Charlotte didn't know what to do.

She wasn't sure if she should comfort Jesse or pretend she didn't see the emotion all over her face.

Before Charlotte had time to make a decision, Jesse said, "That's kind of you to offer, but ..." She looked toward the door, the movement sending a tear down her cheek. "I have an appointment I need to go to, so I don't have time for lunch."

This was the first time Charlotte had seen her cry in their home.

"I have to go," Jesse said, giving Charlotte a final look.

And then she was gone.

Charlotte glanced back at her monitor, remembering the project she had been working on before Jesse knocked. Even though the soil reports had to be submitted to the county today, Charlotte couldn't focus on the numbers that needed to be computed. She couldn't focus on anything.

Besides Jesse.

FORTY-THREE
JESSE
AFTER

AFTER A DAY OF SHOPPING, Viv and I returned to our brownstone where she placed everything I'd bought her on top of her bed. With all the clothes and accessories she'd gotten, not an inch of her comforter was showing. We stood in front of it all, staring at the items. While she was probably putting outfits together in her head, I was looking for a place to sit.

There weren't any chairs in her bedroom.

I couldn't stand for another second.

I went over to the edge of the mattress and said, "You know you've scored when Mom has to move things to make room to sit down," before I took over the small corner. I smiled, trying to hide the pain on my face.

But it was getting harder and harder.

And today had been the roughest so far.

The walking and carrying bags, the sitting and standing—all of it had put such a strain on my body. It would take everything I had just to get up.

Still, it was worth it. Every ache, every painful breath—I

would endure it for the rest of my life if it meant more time with my family.

But choosing torture wasn't even an option.

Not with this disease.

"We're going to need a U-Haul to move it all into my dorm," Viv joked, lifting a pair of earrings off the mattress. She held them up to her ears. "Mom, I can't believe you got me all of this."

I'd spent an obscene amount of money on her today. It was excessive, much more than I'd intended, but once she tried on the first outfit, I forgot it all had a price. And, instead, I had taken in every minute I had with her because … we were almost running out of them.

I wouldn't be at her college graduation.

I wouldn't see the first wrinkle cross her face.

I wouldn't hear the words, *I'm pregnant*.

I wouldn't get to watch her be a mother.

My future was gone.

And I would do anything—absolutely anything—to reverse my sentence.

But, within a few years, my lungs would begin to shut down, and not even a ventilator would keep me alive.

Oh God.

The emotion was in my throat. There was nothing I could do to conceal it at this point. I did the only thing I could, which was embrace it. "I'm going to miss you so much." Tears slowly trickled into my eyes, but it was the right moment for them.

And, as Viv looked at me from the end of the bed, her own eyes began to water. "Mom …" She joined me, sitting on a stack of shirts. "My dorm is only four miles from here. I'm going to see you guys all the time."

You'll see them, baby.

But not me.

"Of course you will," I whispered, my hands shaking too badly to wipe my own cheeks.

I needed to look away.

I needed to pull myself together.

I needed to find my mask.

Since I still didn't have the energy to get up, the only thing I could do was turn my face. So, I focused on the pillow behind me and slid it further away to give me more room. Now that I could stretch out, my body was screaming to lie down. This time, I didn't bother to move anything out of the way. The back of my head sank into the fluffy down, and I spread across all the clothes in my path, searching for a comfortable spot. One that would ease the cramping, that would lessen the tightening in my legs.

"You wore me out today," I moaned. Both kids thought Emery and I were old, so this news wouldn't come as a surprise. I tapped the spot next to me. "Come here, baby."

She lay back and rested into my side, and I pressed my lips to the top of her head, leaving them there while I breathed her in.

Seventeen years.

That was all the time I'd had with her.

It wasn't enough.

There was so much more I wanted to say, wanted to do, wanted to teach her.

"Viv ..." I swallowed. It burned as though I were holding a lit match above my tongue. "Promise me something." My hand went to her cheek, and I did everything I could to hide the tremors. "Promise me you'll always make smart choices." I smelled her shampoo and the perfume she'd tried on at one of the stores and the scent of the restaurant we'd eaten at for lunch. "Because, once you go off to college, we won't be there to protect you ..." The knot was too big. I couldn't talk past it.

She turned her head to look at me. "You don't have to worry; I'm going to make you proud."

This was the moment she would remember for the rest of her life.

How do I make it last as long as possible?

How do I tell my daughter everything she needs to hear without it sounding like a good-bye?

My hand squeezed her face even tighter. "Baby, you've already made us so proud." My lips returned to the top of her head, and I closed my eyes. Minutes passed before I said, "I've been thinking about this a lot, and I've decided I'm going to text you every morning before my bike ride. It'll be early, and I don't expect you to reply. It's just something ... I have to do for me." I inhaled as deeply as I could, the quivers convulsing in my throat. "The same way I walk into your room every morning before you get up for school."

"That's one thing I didn't inherit from you." She laughed.

I was the only morning person in our house—a fact that became an ongoing joke in our family. I appreciated the humor now more than ever.

Just as I was licking the saltiness from my lips, stopping the drips from falling on her head, she locked her fingers with mine.

It caused me to shake even harder, and I was petrified she'd feel it.

I only had a few seconds before I had to pull out of her grasp.

In that time, every word mattered, so I said the ones that meant the most, "I love you, Viv."

"Love you, Mom."

I squeezed her, feeling the strain in my arm, the throbbing in my shoulder, and then I released her. My hand fell to my side, each muscle clenching.

While the pain shot through me, I repeated, *I love you*, in my head. *I love you so much. Don't ever forget that, baby.*

If you need me, I'll be right here. Inside your heart. When you feel that special warmth, just know it's me, hugging you from above, the same way your papa is there for me.

As another streak of wetness marred my cheek, I heard, "*Mooom*," come from the hallway.

"We're in here," Viv replied.

Before Tommy appeared, I used my shoulder to quickly wipe my face, and then I forced a smile across it. "Hi, baby," I said when he appeared in the doorway.

"What are you guys doing?" he asked, moving inside.

While Viv and I had been shopping for college, he'd spent the day with Emery at the Museum of Fine Arts. That was Tommy's favorite place in the city.

It was also one of mine.

"We're relaxing," I answered. I patted the bed. "Climb over the clothes and join us."

Instead of using the pillow Viv and I were sharing, Tommy rested his head on my shoulder. I kissed his forehead but kept my hand at my side. I didn't have the strength to lift it.

"How was the museum?" I asked.

"So fun." His voice sounded like pure energy. I wished I could swallow some. "There was this light installation thing hanging from the ceiling. It was so cool. Someday, I want to make one just like it."

"You will," I said softly. "You're so talented. One day, your art is going to be in that museum."

"You really think so?" he asked.

"Not think. We know," Viv replied before I had the chance.

She had so much love for her brother, and he just idolized her. As an only child, that was a bond I'd yearned for my whole life, but I never imagined anything as strong as the one between Viv and Tommy.

They had been there for each other when my father died.

And they would be there for each other again when I was gone.

I pressed my mouth into Tommy's hair. "My baby boy," I murmured in the same spot I had kissed my daughter. "Being an artist is going to test you; it's going to make you question your talent and fill you with an immense amount of doubt. Don't let fear break you. Use it to make you stronger." I glanced at Viv. "Just don't you dare give up."

"Listen to your mom," Emery said from the doorway. We all looked in his direction as he continued, "Because she's right."

His hands were gripping the molding above the door, and a smile was starting at just the corners of his eyes.

"Come here," I called to my husband. "Join us."

He walked to the edge of the bed, standing just by our feet.

He was so handsome that it hurt. So kind that I felt my heart tremble. So tenacious that I felt his grasp even though he wasn't touching me.

Viv snuggled closer to me, which opened more space for

Emery. Once he lay next to her, I turned my neck, and our eyes connected. He reached across to put his hand on my face, drying my cheek with his palm. He didn't ask why there were tears. He knew.

Except ... he couldn't be more wrong.

FORTY-FOUR
EMERY

I STOOD in the doorway of our bedroom, watching my beautiful wife sleep in our bed. She hadn't heard me come home, nor did Birdie's wagging tail wake her even though the dog was lying across her feet. She just stayed in a fetal position, arms hugging a long pillow as though it were me.

I wasn't surprised she was sleeping even though the clock on her nightstand showed it was only a little past ten. Since Viv had left for college a few weeks ago, Jesse had been going to bed much earlier than normal.

Moving Viv to Boston had been tough on the both of us but especially hard on Jesse. She missed her so much. But my wife wasn't just dealing with Viv being gone. She was helping her mother, she was still mourning the death of her father, she was raising Tommy, and she was dealing with me being in Boston four days a week.

Jesse held us all together. It was no wonder she was so tired.

But that didn't mean I was going to let her sleep. On the

plane ride back to Vermont, she was all I'd thought about. Her mouth. Her body. The warmth that was waiting for me between her legs.

As I moved further into the room, I began taking off my clothes, dropping each piece on the floor, naked by the time I reached the bed.

Birdie lifted her head to greet me, and I patted her before I whispered, "Come on, girl," and pointed to the dog bed on the floor.

She rose from Jesse's feet, and as she jumped off the mattress, I climbed on, taking my wife into my arms, pressing my lips against hers.

She stirred, breathing me in, eventually whispering, "Emery."

"I need you," I said as I pulled away, lifting the long T-shirt over her head, kissing the soft, sweet skin around her collarbone.

I moved further down, taking one of her nipples into my mouth before I slowly parted her legs. Once my face was between them, I licked the inside of each thigh, grazing my nose over her wet skin.

It was a tease and one she was enjoying.

But I didn't rush, nor did I immediately give her the friction she needed.

We had all the time in the world.

So, tonight, I was going to savor my wife.

While her hand raked through my hair, I gently worked her clit. The faster I flicked her, the harder she pulled.

She was falling apart from my tongue, and it was the sexiest fucking sight.

When she shuddered, I drove my fingers in deep, licking

her even quicker than before. Within just a few swipes of my tongue, she was bucking against my face again, and I watched wave after wave pass through her navel. Following each one, she let out a moan.

I lapped up her wetness, waiting for her to still, and then I moved up her body until her legs circled my waist.

"Jesse," I hissed as I gradually buried myself in her heat.

She was close.

She just wasn't close enough.

I reached underneath her and lifted her into my arms, moving us higher on the bed. I then sat with my back against the headboard while she straddled my lap, her arms slipping around my neck. She started slow, finding a rhythm she was comfortable with, and then her riding got deeper and much faster.

She became lost, holding me with a strength I hadn't realized she had, with a look of love in her eyes I hadn't seen lately.

Damn it, I was just as lost.

In the sight of her, in the way her curves looked in the dim light, in the way her breasts bounced each time she fell on me. In the way her head tilted back when her orgasm started to build.

I was right there with her.

My hands went to the center of her back, guiding her closer to me, and I waited for her mouth to land on mine before I groaned, "Baby, you feel so good." My hands wandered lower again, as did my mouth, kissing, caressing, loving every part of my wife's gorgeous body. And, as I breathed, "I love you," across her lips, we broke at the same time.

Her hands gripped me as tightly as she was clenching me

from the inside. "I love you so much more," she whispered, her breath coming out in pants.

Her movements had stopped, and now, she was kissing across my chest, her face hidden behind her hair, so I couldn't see it. But I felt wetness, and I knew it wasn't from her tongue.

"I missed you, Emery."

I hadn't heard the emotion before, but now, it was so clear.

I leaned back, reaching for her face. "Baby, look at me." When she finally gave me her eyes, I continued, "I'm not going anywhere." I wiped the tears, unsure of where they were coming from, but I wasn't going to let her be sad now that I was home.

"It's just been hard."

I had known Viv's absence was going to affect Jesse, so none of this surprised me. I just worried how she was going to hold it together when Tommy was gone.

"I know," I whispered into her mouth. "I miss her, too."

I held her as tightly as I could, waiting for her to calm down, and the second I felt her grip lighten, I lifted her again and set her on the bed with my arms around her. Her breathing eventually evened out, and her eyes dried from the many times I'd wiped them.

And, after several minutes of silence, I broke it and asked, "Are you hungry?" When she didn't say anything, I added, "I brought home a pizza. I figure Tommy can have a slice for breakfast since he was asleep when I got home."

She smiled, but it wasn't nearly as big as usual, and it stopped at her lips, not going any higher. "He's going to love that."

"You will, too. It's margherita, your favorite."

Even with all the exhaustion on her face and the puffy eyes, she nodded. "Maybe I'll have a slice."

I kissed her forehead and said, "I'll be right back," before I got up from the bed.

I threw on a pair of sweats and a T-shirt, and I went into the kitchen. When I returned, I handed her a plate and climbed into the bed beside her.

"*Mmm*," she groaned as she bit into the crust.

I loved how she always started with the back before she moved her way to the point.

"This is perfect ..." Her eyes turned so soft. "Thank you."

I reached toward her and tucked a chunk of hair behind her ear. Once it was out of her face, I still wasn't ready to let go, so I cupped her cheek with my palm.

Since I'd taken on the Boston project, my time had been so limited. When I was home, most of my hours were spent in my office. I was even working weekends just to get everything done.

What was missing was time with my wife.

I didn't pick up my phone to look at my schedule. I just held her face tighter and said, "What are you doing tomorrow?"

As if the question caught her off guard, she put down her half-eaten slice and set the plate on the nightstand. She studied my expression before she answered, "I'm going for a long bike ride in the morning, and then I have a massage at eight, so Luz is going to take Tommy to school." Her stare was boring right through me in a way that told me she was trying to read my thoughts. "Why do you ask?"

I ran my thumb over her bottom lip, brushing off a small crumb. "Will you go to lunch with me?"

That wasn't something I did often unless I was meeting a client. In fact, lunch was a meal I could skip altogether, but it would allow us to be alone, where dinner wouldn't.

She set her hands on her lap and took a deep breath. And, this time, her smile went all the way to the top of her face. "I would love to."

There were tears. I saw them. She just didn't let any of them drip.

FORTY-FIVE
JESSE
AFTER

LIKE THE PAST FIVE MORNINGS, I was awake before my alarm went off. In fact, I hadn't even slept a minute after Emery woke me up to make love. I couldn't close my eyes. I couldn't find a breathing pattern that settled me.

I just rested flat against the bed, my mind an explosion of thoughts, my body tight and throbbing.

I wanted to shut it off.

I wanted to close my eyes.

I wanted to sleep.

I was tired.

God, I was so tired.

The problem was ... I hurt.

Everywhere.

The medications Dr. Moore had prescribed were doing as much as they could, and so was the trial drug I'd started several months ago, hoping it would be a miracle.

My miracle.

But the latest round of testing, which I'd finished the day

before we took Viv to school, showed my ALS was progressing as fast as my doctor had feared.

Nothing could help me at this point. Nothing could stop this monster from destroying me.

All I wanted was time, and I'd give up everything if someone gave me more.

But life wasn't something I could buy or barter.

I sat up a little in bed and looked through the uncovered windows, at the darkness, at the shadows of the mountains that were on the other side of the glass. There was something so welcoming about that view that constantly made me feel like I was home. Even when we traveled to the most beautiful, exotic spots around the world, I always thought of it. Of the cool, vibrant color palette of the rock. Of the snow that lived at the peaks. Of the peacefulness.

Since my diagnosis, it was that peacefulness that kept my mask secure, fastening its thick strap around the back of my head, so it was tied in place.

But the knot was loosening.

The mask was slipping.

And cracks were forming, revealing my face underneath.

I couldn't hide the pain, the tremors, the tightening, the numbness from the paralysis that was setting in.

I was always able to hide it. What'd happened … to me?

I was strong.

I just wasn't that strong anymore.

I turned toward my husband, the man I had called my best friend for twenty-four years, and I ran my hands under my eyes.

There weren't any tears.

There couldn't be from this point going forward.

The small light we kept on in the bathroom gave just enough glow that I could see the outline of his face. On the mornings he was home, before I left for my workout, I would take in his features, just like I was doing now. Eyes that melted me, lips that knew how to heat my entire body.

I placed my hand on his cheek, not worrying about waking him. He was such a sound sleeper; it would take more than my touch to cause his eyes to open.

The whiskers of his beard roughed up my tender skin. It was fall, which meant he was starting to grow it out, entering my favorite season.

The strands would soon be longer and thicker, and he would rub them against my cheek after he kissed me, knowing how much I enjoyed it.

God, he was such a good man.

Honest.

Loyal.

Trustworthy.

I didn't know how I'd gotten so lucky. How fate had made our paths cross that day my freshman year at Northeastern.

I'd been walking back to my dorm after leaving the library, and he was returning from lacrosse practice. We reached the entrance of the building at the same time, and he swiped his college ID across the reader and opened the door for me.

It was his smile. That was what captured me first, and I stared at it the whole way through the lobby. I lived on the second floor, too short of a distance to take the elevator. But Emery was on the fourth, a fact I had learned my first week there when I saw this cute boy from afar and quietly inquired about him.

For some reason, he'd followed me into the stairwell that day.

And, from that moment, Emery became my entire life.

I'm sorry.

I'm so fucking sorry.

"I love you," I whispered.

Even though he didn't hear me, the words still needed to come out of my mouth, the same way I said them every morning at this exact time.

I had two minutes before I needed to change my clothes, so I stayed just like this and didn't let go. I didn't talk either. I just held my husband, and thoughts began to pop in my head. Of the pictures that were framed around the house, of the wall of selfies that hung in my library. Of the places we'd visited. Of the stories we'd shared with each other.

Of the memories.

Of the smiles.

There were so many smiles.

You have my permission.

I wanted so badly to say that to him.

I couldn't.

I didn't have it in me. I could do so much ... but not that.

At exactly two minutes, I released his face and changed into a pair of compression pants, a fleece, and a headband made of the same material. Then, I put on a pair of sneakers, grabbed my phone, and went to Emery's side of the bed. He hadn't moved in the short time I was gone. His expression was so peaceful, like the mountains on the other side of the window.

I had only fifteen seconds to spare.

Just like I did every time I left, I leaned into his face and pressed my lips against his cheek. I breathed him in. And, in the quietest voice, I said, "See you later, my angel."

I moved to the end of the bed where Birdie slept. She'd lasted about an hour on her dog bed before she jumped back in ours and took up the bottom section by my feet. When I reached her, I ducked down, putting my nose against hers. We stayed that way for only a second before her tongue licked all the way up to my forehead.

If I talked to her, she would get excited and stand up. So, I kissed her on the top of the head, and I hurried out of our room, going down the long hallway to the kids' wing. Only one of the rooms was occupied, and that was the door I opened. Tommy was on his stomach in the middle of the bed. He slept like a bear; it would take shaking and some shouting before he heard me.

Twice a week, on the days I got a massage, I didn't take him to school, and I wouldn't see him again until I picked him up later in the afternoon. That was why, on these mornings, I always came in to kiss him.

I sat on the side of his bed and put my hand on his back. There weren't words strong enough to describe my love for this boy. Nothing I could voice or show him would ever define it. It was just something he had to believe.

Something he had to feel.

And I knew he did.

"Be you," I whispered.

That was all I wanted—for him not to be influenced by others, not to lose who he was. Not to mimic or feel jealous or inadequate. I just wanted him to be him.

I rubbed a circle over his warm skin, and then I slowly pushed myself to my feet, making sure I was steady and wouldn't fall before I leaned down to kiss his forehead. "I love you."

My mouth stayed pressed against my son for several more beats as I inhaled as much of his scent as I could, and then I went out the door. On my way to the garage, I typed Viv a text just like I had done yesterday at this time and the day before.

Me: Good morning, baby. I love you so much. xoxo

I kept my phone in my hand because there was one more message I needed to send. This one was to my mom. She wasn't that savvy with her smartphone, and I worried the sound of a text would wake her. I was sure her e-mails had a quieter notification, if one at all, so this was the safest way to communicate.

I'd call if it wasn't so early, but I know you're still sleeping. I'm going to have lunch with Emery at noon, and then I'll be over. I'll ask Luz to make us something sweet that I can bring with me. Love you.

I zipped my cell into the small pocket in my pants, and I entered the garage. I put on my helmet and walked the bike to the base of the driveway before I straddled it.

The pitch-black air was so brisk that I could see my breath. Fall in Vermont could sometimes be as cold as winter. My body shook from the temperature, which was wreaking havoc with my muscles, but I knew, once I started pedaling, I would warm.

Just as I was about to kick off, I felt something in my chest.

It was as though someone had reached through my skin and clenched my heart and shook it in their fist.

How could I have forgotten?

I took out my phone, pulled up the last text I'd sent Bay, and began typing.

Me: I'm going to the library today. I know you can't meet me there, but I'll be thinking of you while I'm reading the classics. Love you, Bay. So much.

Once the message was sent, I deleted the thread, and then I did the same to her information that was saved in my Contacts. And, as the tension left my chest, I zipped my phone in my pocket, and I pushed off, both feet now on the pedals.

Six miles.

That was the route I used to take when I biked or ran every day. Except it had been months since I did either.

My family thought that was what I did every morning. What they didn't realize was, since shortly after my diagnosis, I would take the bike to the guesthouse on the other side of the property where I read for an hour before I drenched myself in the sink and returned home.

But I needed the road. I needed to find me again. I needed that peacefulness I felt when I looked at the mountains, believing I would find the same thing once I got reacquainted with my bike.

As soon as I began to pedal, it was like being back with an old friend. I knew every turn, bump.

I wasn't worried about the course. I could do this route with my eyes closed.

I feared my body couldn't handle the distance.

I'd lost my endurance. My steady breathing. The atrophy in my muscles becoming much more pronounced.

Today, that wasn't going to be a problem.

Because, today, I was a warrior.

And, no matter what ... I would be fine.

FORTY-SIX
EMERY

I WAS STANDING in the kitchen, reaching inside the fridge, when I heard the sound of the doorbell.

"I'll get it," Charlotte said before I had a chance to turn around.

I thanked her and grabbed the bottle of water I'd been aiming for and shut the door. As I opened the cap, I checked the clock on the microwave.

Last night, Jesse had told me the time of her massage appointment. I just couldn't remember what she'd said. However, I was sure it was earlier this morning since she had agreed to go to lunch at noon.

And that was only fifteen minutes from now.

"Emery," Charlotte said as she appeared in the archway of the kitchen.

I glanced away from the microwave, and my eyes connected with hers. Her face was stark white ... and she wasn't alone.

Two police officers stood behind her.

"They'd like to talk to you," she said. She joined me on the other side of the island, standing right next to me, as the officers moved closer.

I didn't like their expressions or that they were in my house in the first place. A visit from the police was never a good thing.

"What's going on?" I asked them.

"Mr. Black," one of them started, halting just in front of the island, "we have some unfortunate news."

While he paused, my arms crossed over my chest, and I backed up until the counter hit the top of my ass. I was bracing myself for what he was about to say.

"It's difficult to say this, so I'm just going to be frank. We believe we found your wife at the bottom of the mountain."

Charlotte gasped.

It was a sound I'd never forget. Like the noise a metal beam made when it was dropped from a crane at eighty feet. And then would come the vibration from the metal, the earth shaking while it absorbed the impact, the same way my feet were trembling right now.

My arms dropped, my hands reaching behind me to grip the counter. "Where is she?" The pounding in my heart was making it hard to speak. "You said you found my wife at the bottom of the mountain, so where the hell is she? At the hospital? On her way there? Where do I need to drive to go see her?"

"Emery ..." Charlotte whispered.

I didn't understand why her face was so white, why there was sadness in her eyes, why she wasn't trying to press the cops for more information so that I could get my ass to Jesse.

"I'm sorry, Mr. Black," one of the cops said. "She's at the morgue."

"She …" I breathed, my head swinging toward the officer who had just spoken. "She …" I tried again. But my mouth shut. There wasn't any air to get even a single word out.

She …

As in …

My wife.

"Please tell us what happened," Charlotte said.

All I saw was black.

All I felt was numbness.

I wasn't even sure if I was still standing in the kitchen.

"We believe she tried to stop as she was biking down the hill. We assume she took the turn too fast, and her bike hit the guardrail."

She'd gone for a bike ride this morning.

She went for one every morning.

My wife.

No.

This was impossible.

They were confused. They had it all wrong. There was no fucking way the woman they were talking about was my Jess.

I couldn't stand here. I had to do something.

I had to …

I lifted my foot and didn't feel the floor beneath me when I took a step. I didn't know where I was headed, and I couldn't even see, but that didn't stop me from pacing forward again. This time, a wave of air passed through me. My ankle wobbled.

Fuck.

And, suddenly, I felt myself falling.

"I've got you," Charlotte said as she gripped my arm, holding me up.

I couldn't feel her, but I knew she was there. Someone was because I wasn't standing on my own.

I was …

On the mountain.

At the guardrail.

My tires rounding the edge of the rock.

My fucking heart.

"I'm sorry, Mr. Black," one of the officers said.

And then the other one added, "We're going to need you to come to the morgue to identify the body. We were able to trace her through her cell phone, but she didn't have any ID on her, so we don't have a positive identification."

I opened my mouth.

Not a goddamn thing came out of it.

I had …

Nothing.

"We'll follow you over there, Officer," Charlotte said, now steering me toward the counter. "Just give us a few minutes, and we'll meet you outside."

I heard them leave, and then I felt her shake my arm.

"Emery …"

I couldn't look up.

I couldn't even move.

"Emery …" Charlotte's voice grew louder each time.

But I was locked from the inside. The only thing that would release me was if someone told me my wife wasn't at the morgue. If they said this was a massive misunderstanding and the cops had stopped at the wrong house.

If they told me my wife was going to walk through the front door at any goddamn second.

"Emery, please look at me."

Her voice was full of emotion, and it was stern at the same time. Enough so that it caused me to lift my head. None of the color had returned to her face. It was still ghostly white, and there were tears in her eyes.

For a second, I wanted to ask her what they were from and why she was so upset.

And then I remembered.

And then it hit me all over again.

I can't fucking take this.

"The police are waiting for us outside," she said.

She stood close, and I saw her gripping me, but I still didn't feel it.

"We're going to get in my car, and I'm going to drive us there, okay?"

I didn't know how I was going to get in her car, never mind carry through with anything else she'd just said.

"We need to leave, Emery," she told me, and she began to lead me to the door.

After a few steps, I stopped. I had to know something before we moved another inch. Before I left the house and faced this. "Is it her, Charlotte? Is it really my wife that's dead in the morgue?"

She clutched my hand, and after a few breaths, she said, "Whatever happens today, you're going to get through it."

When Charlotte shifted into park, I was staring through the

windshield from the passenger seat of her car. I hadn't spoken since we left the house.

I had tried and couldn't.

That wasn't the only thing wrong.

From the moment she'd brought the police into my home, I had been forgetting large chunks of time. My body was going through the motions. My mind was far away.

And, suddenly, I would come into consciousness, like now, while we were standing in this cold room. I didn't remember coming inside, if I had spoken to anyone, if I'd filled out paperwork.

But there were white walls around me. I was fucking freezing, and all I could smell was an intense aroma of formaldehyde.

My eyes fell onto the table in front of me. There was a person on top of it, covered with a white sheet. I could see nothing besides the outline of the body, and based on the size, it was female.

Charlotte was holding my arm again.

I didn't tell her to let go.

The truth was, I didn't know if I could do this without someone holding on to me.

"Mr. Black, I'm going to pull back the sheet," a man wearing a white coat said.

I didn't respond. I had nothing in me to even nod.

But I held my breath, and my entire body shook.

The first thing I saw was brown hair.

A fair-skinned forehead.

Brows that arched over the most gorgeous, piercing blue eyes.

Except they were closed ... and her red lips had a touch of blue to them.

Her hands were at her sides, bloody, banged up, several of her nails gone.

She was missing a sneaker.

Where is her goddamn sneaker?

Her foot was probably cold.

My wife's feet were always cold, and I was constantly wrapping my hands around them to warm them.

But, now, her toes were as blue as her lips.

Jesus, Jesse.

I took a step forward, feeling a tightening on my arm, and I ignored it to surround my wife's foot with my hands. To warm them. To make her feel me.

I rubbed my thumb up and down her arches.

Usually, she groaned when I did this.

I heard nothing.

Besides Charlotte whispering, "Emery, look at me."

As I glanced up, I caught Jesse's face. It wasn't the first time I'd seen it since the guy in the white coat pulled back the sheet. This was just the first time I realized what the hell I was looking at.

Baby ...

You're really gone.

Bile rose to the back of my throat.

I looked for a trash can. Since I didn't see one, I got out of Charlotte's hold and rushed to the side of the room where there was a sink, and I leaned over it and threw up.

The back of my throat burned; my insides felt like they were tearing apart.

When the heaving finally stopped, I turned on the water and stuck my mouth underneath it, filling my cheeks to cool down the fire in my mouth. I shut off the water and saw Charlotte and the man in the white coat were standing only a few feet from me.

"Emery, the police are going to take you home," Charlotte said.

She handed me a paper towel and urged me to wipe my mouth. I dried off my lips, and then I squeezed the wet paper into my palm.

"Once I leave here, I'm going to pick up Tommy from school, and I'll bring him to you."

Tommy.

Viv.

Fuck.

"But, before I do that, there's some paperwork I have to sign first," she continued. "Once it's finished, I'll grab your son, and you can tell him and Viv the news."

Take me home.

To our house.

That won't have Jesse in it.

Because the news she wanted me to deliver was that ... Jesse was dead.

I wanted to go over to that table, crawl on top of it, lift my wife into my arms, and ask her why we weren't going for lunch.

And, just as I was about to go do that, Charlotte said to the guy in the white coat, "I'll be right back." Her arm then circled my back, and she moved with me through the cold room, down a hallway, and past what appeared to be a lobby.

There were several police officers standing outside.

"I'll see you in a few hours," she said to me when one of them approached.

I didn't know if it was the one from earlier. I just saw a shiny name tag and badge. I heard him give me his condolences.

And then the last thing I remembered him saying was, "Come with me, Mr. Black."

FORTY-SEVEN
CHARLOTTE

CHARLOTTE HELD her phone to her ear, and as the agent from the private airline picked up, she said, "This is Charlotte Scott, calling on behalf of Mr. Emery Black. I would like to reserve a plane for Emery's daughter, Viv Black, departing Boston at four o'clock this afternoon and landing in Burlington."

Charlotte was standing in the hallway, directly outside the room where Jesse's body was being examined. She was pacing between the two doors. Every time she caught a peek of Jesse's skin, something inside of Charlotte would break, and she'd turn and walk in the opposite direction.

"Let me check availability," the agent said. "Please hold for just a moment."

Charlotte had taken ecstasy once in college. She remembered the way it'd made her heart race, how her senses were on overdrive, her emotions surging on a scale unlike anything she'd ever experienced before.

That was how Charlotte felt right now. She was tingling from the inside out, unable to stop moving, sensitive to everything around her.

"Viv is all set for four p.m. tonight," the agent said when she returned to the line. "Is there anything else I can help you with, Charlotte?"

"No, thank you," Charlotte said and hung up.

When she reached the door farthest from the exam room, she turned one last time to head back inside. But, just as she got to the entrance, she saw one of the police officers who had come to Emery's house was now standing with the medical examiner, and they were looking at Jesse.

"Isn't this an interesting situation?" the cop said.

Charlotte stayed to the side of the doorway—within range of hearing their conversation and where she could see both of them.

"Why is that?" the medical examiner replied.

The officer walked to the top of Jesse's head and looked down at her face. "The housekeeper said she was an experienced biker and had biked those roads for years. She would have known how fast to take the turns, and she was going double the speed."

The medical examiner had a tablet in his hand, his attention shifting from the screen to Jesse as though he were taking an inventory. "We get several of these cases every year, same scenario. They get tired or cramp up. Anything can take place when they're going that fast, and the visibility isn't great because it's still dark out. It only takes a second to lose control."

The cop shook his head. "But she knew this area so well ..."

The medical examiner fixed his gaze on the cop. "I know what you're inferring, and we see plenty of those cases, too." The tablet dropped to his side. "Listen, I haven't even started the exam, but let me show you some things I see right off the bat." He pointed at Jesse's hand. "That kind of damage doesn't happen to someone who bikes over the edge of a mountain because they don't want to live anymore."

"No?"

He walked the officer over to Jesse's other side where there was a gaping wound in her palm and two of her fingers were missing. "Injuries like this happen when someone is clinging to the guardrail and then hanging on to the edge of the mountain for dear life, bearing their own weight to the point where their fingers start to snap off."

"Or to a woman really trying to cover her tracks."

The medical examiner took a step back. "Were there brake marks on the pavement?"

The cop nodded, proving the medical examiner's point even further. "Then, you know this has accidental death written all over it."

Charlotte had heard enough and stepped into the room. The sound of her boots caused both men to look in her direction. As she walked toward them, she ignored the body on the table and said, "Is the paperwork ready for me to sign?"

The moment she had seen Emery grab Jesse's foot, she had known he was in no condition to be here, let alone sign the documents required when identifying a body. He needed to be home with his kids.

Charlotte was going to make that happen.

She had scheduled Viv's flight a little later in the day to

give Emery plenty of time to tell her. Before he broke the news to either of his children, he needed to get himself together. While he was off doing that, Charlotte was going to be picking up the pieces one by one, starting with what needed to be done here.

"Yes," the medical examiner said, lifting a folder off the counter. He opened the flap, took out several sheets, and spread them across the countertop. He set a pen next to them. "Each one needs your signature."

As Charlotte moved over to him, she tried so hard not to look at Jesse. She'd done enough of that when she came into the room with Emery, and she certainly didn't need the reminder.

Because it was a sight she would remember for the rest of her life.

But it was too hard to look away, and she found herself taking in Jesse's hands and her face.

Her bare foot.

A sob began to form in her gut, churning its way up her stomach and into her throat.

She couldn't let it out. Not here. But she would as soon as she got into her car. There, she would have several minutes alone where she could gather herself before she picked up Tommy.

Based on the way she felt right now, she would need every one.

Charlotte stood in the kitchen, staring at the back of Emery's and Tommy's heads as they sat on the couch in the living room.

Since Emery had informed him of his mother's passing, the two of them hadn't moved.

Charlotte felt helpless.

She had no idea how to get Tommy to stop crying, how to make Emery feel better. How to soothe Viv's screams because that was all she had done on the phone once Emery gave her the news.

Viv was due in soon, and Charlotte couldn't imagine how intense the emotions were going to be when the three of them were together.

So far, she'd watched it all go down from the sidelines, like she was still doing now. She just didn't know her place; she didn't know what to do with herself.

The only thing she knew was to stay busy.

She turned around and began collecting the ingredients she needed to bake bread—the one thing that always made her feel better. Since Luz went to the farmers market every other morning, there was plenty of fresh fruits and vegetables to add in.

Charlotte went with her favorite flavor.

One she hadn't made in a while.

She didn't speak as she prepared the mixture. She didn't even look up from the counter unless it was to glance at the stove. She fully immersed herself, getting lost in the steps, repeating them each time she finished a batch.

When there were six loaves on the drying rack, Luz and Viv were just walking in from the airport. Since Emery couldn't drive, Charlotte had thought the next most familiar face should go.

That was Luz.

Viv walked as far as the counter, directly across from

where Charlotte stood, and she stared at the back of her father's and brother's heads. Emery's arm was across Tommy's shoulders, and their temples were resting against each other. On the TV in front of them was a movie Emery had shot of the whole family on vacation. The kids looked much younger. Charlotte suspected it was from around ten years ago.

Every few seconds, there was a direct view of Jesse where she would be speaking.

Every time, Viv's shoulders would shake a little harder.

Her father was unaware she was even home because she hadn't made a sound.

Charlotte remembered when her own mother had died a few years after she graduated college. Charlotte's relationship with her had been much different than the one Viv had had with Jesse. Still, she could recall how much that phone call had hurt and what it was like to return to her mom's apartment in Florida to bury her.

Back then, Charlotte would have done anything for a set of arms to wrap around her. It wouldn't have mattered whose they were. She'd just wanted to be comforted.

That was why Charlotte left the loaves of bread cooling on the counter and moved over to Viv, wrapping her arms around Jesse's daughter.

And she squeezed the young girl with everything she had.

Viv didn't push her away. She didn't say a word either. She just slowly began to unravel. First, by not being able to hold her own weight and then breaking down in tears.

While Emery stayed on the couch, hugging his son, Charlotte clutched his daughter. Charlotte didn't let go, gripping Viv with everything she had so that Viv wouldn't fall, her shoulder absorbing every tear that dripped from Viv's eyes.

Even if that meant staying in this position for hours, Charlotte would.

All Charlotte wanted was to be here for this family.

Because, after today, none of them would ever be the same.

Not even her ...

FORTY-EIGHT
CHARLOTTE

AFTER CHARLOTTE HAD LEFT the morgue, she had gone to her house and packed enough for a week's stay before she went to pick up Tommy from school. She'd had a feeling she would have a few rough days ahead of her, and the Blacks would need her to stay overnight.

She was right.

Jesse had died three days ago, and Charlotte hadn't been home even once. She moved straight into the Blacks' guest room, and she worked around the clock to make sure the family had everything.

Emotions were high, as she'd suspected, and Emery was barely keeping it together. Luz was doing everything she could to help, but she was crying as often as the kids.

Charlotte became the strength they all needed.

Luz cooked the food, and Charlotte made sure everyone ate, that they showered. She was there when one of them needed to be held.

Even Emery.

Since Jesse's accident, he hadn't gone into his office once, so Charlotte was also managing everything in his absence along with all the arrangements for the funeral. No one was in the right frame of mind to make those decisions. Charlotte made them for Emery and his mother-in-law, gladly taking the stress off their backs.

The second she opened her eyes the morning of the funeral, Charlotte could sense the heartbreak everyone was feeling in the house. As soon as she got dressed, she checked on Tommy and did a quick errand before she went into the master wing.

She didn't have to knock; the door was already open. She still carefully walked in just in case Emery was undressed. Within a few steps, she heard the sound of the shower.

The first thing she did was look at the bed. There weren't any clothes lying on top of it, so she went into his closet to see what he had picked out to wear. Nothing was hanging on his valet rod.

She would fix that.

She went over to his suits and chose a black one with a white pinstripe shirt and a black silk tie. She even took out a pair of shoes and set them on the floor in front of his suit.

A neighbor had prescribed Emery a month's worth of Xanax. She kept the bottle in her purse and fed them to her boss when enough time had gone by, making sure he stayed far below the maximum dosage for the day.

He was hurting, but she wasn't going to lose him, too.

She left one of the pills on the island in his closet with a small bottle of water.

It was going to be a long day, and this would help him get through it, especially since the wake was following the funeral and it was being held at the house. She had hired a caterer, who had arrived early this morning, prepping food for all the people who would be attending.

Since she had baked twelve loaves of pound cake the night Jesse died, she gave them to the caterer to use as part of the dessert. It would be served with an assortment of cookies and brownies.

And, since it was Charlotte's favorite flavor, it felt even more special.

Now that Emery had everything he needed, she left his room and went into the kids' wing. She had already helped Tommy find something to wear the night before, and she'd found him showered and dressed earlier this morning. She was sure he was in the kitchen now, where Luz was making him something to eat.

She didn't think Luz's attempt would work, but she insisted on trying. If the kids refused the bacon and eggs, Charlotte had a plan. But, first, she had to check on Viv. She knocked on her door, and after several more attempts with no response, she tried the knob. It was unlocked, and she found Viv in a bathrobe, standing in the middle of her closet with her back facing the entrance.

"I have nothing to wear to my mother's funeral," Viv said. She didn't turn around when she spoke. And, since there wasn't a mirror in here, Viv had no idea who was even standing behind her.

"I'll help you find something," Charlotte said, rushing inside the large space, stopping at the first rack. There were several dresses. The first dress was black and had a fitted, long-sleeved bodice with a billowy bottom. Charlotte held it up and said, "How about this one?"

Viv crossed her arms over her chest and shook her head. "Mom bought me that right before I left for college, and I forgot to bring it with me to Boston. I can't wear that ... it doesn't feel right."

She remembered when she had stood in front of her own closet, choosing an outfit to wear to her mother's funeral. She recalled the pressure she'd felt to pick the right dress. Even though her sister and a few friends would be the only people attending, it'd mattered to Charlotte what she looked like that day.

The same way it mattered to Viv.

She put the dress back and sifted through a few more, coming across a navy one. It was strapless and paired with a matching cardigan. She showed it to Viv.

"I wore that to my pre-graduation ceremony. I ... can't."

She said nothing as she hung it back up and moved on to the next section of clothes. Within a few swipes, she came across a black dress that wrapped across the front and tied at the waist. It was simple, appropriate. She lifted the hanger and turned around.

Viv gave it a once-over, and her eyes went wide, tears immediately dripping from them. "Oh my God," she whispered. She covered her face with her hands and started to sob.

She put the dress back and hurried to Viv's side, throwing her arms around the girl's thin frame. "*Shh*," she sang in an attempt to calm her. "You're okay."

It didn't matter how much she swayed or how tightly she squeezed; Viv continued to cry.

"Do you want to tell me what made you so upset?"

"I-it's not m-mine," Viv stuttered as she tried to breathe through each cry.

She leaned back, so she could see Viv's face and brushed away several hairs that were stuck to it. "Whose is it, sweetheart?" Charlotte then worked off some of the makeup that had streaked down Viv's cheeks.

"It's m-my mom's," she said so softly.

Charlotte felt a knot lodge into the back of her throat.

She took a deep breath, reminding herself that she needed to push her feelings aside. "I think you should wear the first black dress I showed you." She ran her thumbs under Viv's eyes, wiping away the eyeliner. "I know your mom bought it for you not that long ago, but maybe that's all the more reason to wear it since you know how much she loved it on you."

Viv's lips quivered. "We had so much fun that day." Her eyes closed as though she were remembering it. "I dragged her all over the city, and she never complained even though she hated to shop."

Charlotte had flown in at the end of their trip to work with Emery. She'd never forget the amount of shopping bags that had lined the stairwell. She'd certainly never seen that many before.

"I think you should wear the dress, Viv. It will look beautiful on you, and I think it would mean a lot to your mom." When Viv finally nodded, Charlotte added, "Once you get dressed, I'll fix your makeup, and then we'll grab you something to eat before we go."

"I'm not hungry."

She'd had a feeling that was going to be the case; it just wasn't a feeling she had come up with on her own. "I stopped by McDonald's this morning and grabbed you a milkshake," Charlotte said, setting her hand on top of Viv's shoulder. "A vanilla one, your favorite kind. Maybe you could get down a few sips of it?"

She had picked up a vanilla one for Emery and chocolate for Tommy and herself. She'd drunk hers on the way back to the Blacks' house, having to pull over before she reached their street when she got the urge to throw up.

"I'll try," Viv replied.

"Great." Charlotte left her for just a second to get the dress and bring it over to her. "Put this on and meet me in your bathroom."

Viv looked at the hanger dangling from Charlotte's finger, but she didn't take it from her. And, a second later, a new streak of eyeliner began to stain her cheek. "I'm not going to make it through today."

Charlotte pulled Viv into her arms once more and hugged her with everything she had. "You're absolutely going to make it through today, and you're going to be strong for Tommy because he needs his big sister so badly right now."

"I ... can't."

Charlotte sighed, clutching the girl with all of her strength. "I know it feels that way right now, but all the people who will be there today have so much love for your mom." Her voice turned to a whisper. "Take all of that love, Viv. It will help you; trust me." She released her just enough to look at her face. "I know it feels impossible right now, but I've gone through it. I know exactly how you're feeling, and I know you're going to survive this. It's going to hurt like hell, but you're going to be all right." Charlotte held on for a little longer, and then she hooked the hanger on to Viv's palm and took a few steps toward the bathroom. "Meet me in there when you're dressed."

She shut the door behind her, and as she waited, she got out a washcloth. While that was soaking in warm water in the sink, she found some tinted moisturizer and lip gloss and set those on the counter. Since Viv still hadn't joined her, she took out her phone and started to clean out Emery's inbox, responding to the messages that needed immediate answers.

She wanted to sit and take a second, knowing how challenging today was going to be, but she was worried about the thoughts in her head. The last time she had let her brain really go there, diving into the layers of the last few days, it had made her sick.

So, she focused on Emery's e-mail, and when Viv finally joined her, she made sure Viv didn't leave the bathroom with a speck of black streaks on her face.

Charlotte wondered what Jesse would think if she were looking down ...

As soon as the wake started, Charlotte found herself in the kitchen. She wanted to make sure the caterer was doing everything she'd been hired to, and she wanted to give the family time to be with their friends.

She hadn't had any alcohol to drink in the last three days, not even a sip of wine during the moments she thought she was going to break. But it was time, and she poured herself a glass of red and stood in the corner to drink it, hoping she'd be able to keep it down.

She could hear Jesse's friends on the other side of the wall. There was a group of them sitting at a table. She'd met them several times when Jesse had them over. She'd hugged them at the funeral.

That was as close as Charlotte wanted to get.

She had barely made a dent in her glass when the caterer came over, setting two cookies down in front of her.

"You haven't eaten anything all day. You've been too busy serving everyone else." She nodded toward the plate. "Eat up; you need the sugar."

The caterer had witnessed Tommy refusing to eat Luz's bacon and eggs and how reluctant the family was with the milkshakes, eventually trying them and getting at least half of the medium size down.

As for Charlotte, she had no interest in putting anything in her stomach besides the pinot noir in her hand. The thought alone made her want to dry-heave.

"Thank you," Charlotte said, lifting the plate to be nice.

"While I'm over here, do you happen to know if they have a food processor?" the caterer asked. "I've checked the pantry and several of the cabinets. It's hiding from me."

Charlotte had used it to make the pound cake, so she knew exactly where it was. She waved her hand in the air and said, "It's in the dining room—an odd place to keep it, I know. Follow me."

She led the caterer over to the hutch, which was only a few feet from where Jesse's friends were sitting. Now that she was in the room with them, their conversation seemed to die down. Charlotte didn't look in their direction, but she felt their stares as she grabbed the food processor off the bottom shelf.

When she handed it to the caterer, she saw Tommy walk past the dining room, and she caught up to him. She asked him if he needed anything. He didn't, so she went back into the kitchen and returned to her wine.

Emery had designed the most breathtaking house, but he'd made the walls far too thin, which Charlotte learned when she took a sip of wine and she heard Alicia say, "I swear to God, if I didn't know better, I would have thought that was Jesse with her hand on Tommy's shoulder, listening to him so intently."

"Their mannerisms are identical," another woman said.

"It's uncanny," Alicia added.

Charlotte took her drink and walked to the other side of the kitchen.

But she did it with a smile on her face.

FORTY-NINE
EMERY

THREE MONTHS.

That was the amount of time that had passed since I touched my wife. Since she walked out of our home, got on her bike, and never returned.

Whenever I heard a noise, I expected it to be her. If a door opened, I waited for her to walk through it. I looked for her in the house. I woke up in the middle of the night, grabbing for her. I searched for her scent in every room I entered.

She was on my mind.

Constantly.

And, now, everything was different.

Why the fuck isn't she here? Goddamn it!

Shouting those words had done nothing to change the outcome, so I found myself saying them in my head several times a day.

Twenty-four years—that was how long I'd had her.

And then ...

She was gone.

I felt her absence everywhere. In each breath. In my hands when I went to wrap them around her, and all I got was cold air. In her closet when I stepped inside to feel her, and the intensity of her scent was starting to fade.

Part of me had died that day on the mountain.

The part that was alive didn't know how to live without her.

For more than half my life, she had been there to answer every question, fill in the missing pieces of a thought; she had known what I needed before it even occurred to me.

She'd made sure I never wanted for anything.

And, now, I wanted things she couldn't give me, and I didn't know what the fuck to do with myself.

But it wasn't just me.

I had two kids who needed their mother.

I wasn't her.

I couldn't even come close to being her.

I was just a man trying to hold it together, but my goddamn hands were slipping. I wasn't equipped to handle this alone. We were supposed to do this together.

That was what she'd promised.

I'd believed her. I'd counted on her.

Now, I was here without her.

Jesse.

The thought of her name hurt. The sound of it was even worse. Three months later, and the feeling hadn't lessened, but life had to go on. My family needed to get back to their normal routine. That was what my grief counselor had encouraged during our first few sessions.

After being at home for a week, I'd urged Viv to return to college. Tommy had gone back to school.

That was when I'd begun joining Charlotte in the office. I wasn't getting anything done. I wasn't designing. But I was there. At the beginning, that'd felt like a lot.

Now that some time had passed and I could manage my workload again, I was due for a trip to Boston. Luz had offered to stay with Tommy, and his counselor had assured me that my son could handle me being gone for a few days.

I just wasn't ready.

Traveling to our second home was an undertaking I wasn't able to grasp yet even if that meant I'd only be a few miles from Viv.

Because, even though we had returned to normal, there was nothing normal about my life.

Tommy and I ate Luz's meals together, and there were two people missing from the table. I took him to school and made sure his homework was done—things I didn't usually do.

Once I got in my empty bed, my thoughts would keep me up. Not every night, but many. When they did, I would come into my office, the same way I had tonight, and I'd pull up YouTube and watch mindless videos.

I didn't want to think. I didn't want to remember. I didn't want to question.

I just wanted to get lost.

Hours passed.

And, out of nowhere, I heard Charlotte say my name. I looked toward the doorway, and that was where I found her standing, her body leaning against the frame.

It was dark in the office, which told me the sun hadn't risen; therefore, I knew it was before seven and far too early for her to be here.

"Can't sleep?" she asked.

She had her own code; she was allowed to come anytime she wanted. For the first two weeks after Jesse was gone, Charlotte had lived at the house. From the moment the police had rung the doorbell, she'd dropped everything to support my family. I was grateful. In so many fucking ways. But, as much as I wanted her to stay, she had to get back to her life. My family had taken up enough of her time, and it wasn't right to take up any more. She'd stopped staying the night at that point, but she still worked long hours and was here much later than she should be.

Much earlier, too, from the looks of it.

I pushed back in my chair, my hands holding the armrest. "No," I said.

The only light illuminating the room was from my monitor, allowing me to see just a shadow of her. That was all I needed to know it was Charlotte ... and not my wife.

"Have you been getting any sleep at all?" she inquired. "I've been wondering. I've just been afraid to hear your answer."

"A few hours a night."

I wasn't sure if that was the truth.

Most evenings were a blur.

"You're doing such a good job of taking care of the kids," she said, "but you're forgetting about you."

My thumb scratched the armrest like I was picking something off. "I don't know what I'm doing, but it certainly doesn't feel like a good job."

"Stop being so hard on yourself." Her voice was the calmness I'd needed to hear. "Tell me what I can do to make this easier on you."

I shook my head. "Charlotte ..."

My pain was the only thing left to give, and no one could take that from me.

After several seconds, she replied, "Let me help you, Emery."

"*Let me help you,*" repeated in my head over and over as she stepped in my direction, walking around my desk.

I swiveled my chair to meet her, and she stopped right in front of me.

"Tell me what you need," she whispered.

She took another step.

She was close.

The closest she'd ever stood to me.

I didn't know how to respond.

But, when she inhaled, I felt it.

It had been more than twenty-four years since I felt another woman breathe. There had been girlfriends before Jesse, but I barely remembered them.

"Emery, let me"—Charlotte's hand slowly lifted from her side, and I watched it move through the air and very carefully land on my shoulder—"help you."

I wasn't breathing.

The feeling of her was so unfamiliar.

It wasn't Jesse.

But it felt good.

Nothing had felt that way in three months. It had all been torture. Except her hand on me wasn't, and I ... liked it.

The truth of that hurt like hell, especially because my kids couldn't give me that feeling. Not when I heard how much hurt was in Viv's voice and how much I saw in Tommy's expressions.

They were a reminder.

Charlotte wasn't.

"Emery ..." she said again as her arms moved, gradually wrapping around me, pulling me in for a hug. She squeezed me and continued, "Give me your pain."

I thought no one could take it from me, but was that true?

There was a body pressed against me that wasn't my wife's.

Arms that weren't hers.

A face that was as foreign as her scent.

A face ... that was my assistant's.

I didn't know what the fuck to do.

But being in Charlotte's arms was making me feel something I hadn't in three months, and it felt so damn good.

I missed this feeling.

I wanted more.

And I wanted to give her more of my pain.

"Let me help you," she whispered into my neck.

I didn't think.

I'd done enough of that.

Instead, I lifted my hands off my lap, I circled them around her, and I clutched Charlotte with everything I had left.

When I breathed her in, each inhale reminded me of who was in my arms.

Charlotte smelled sweet.

And that was what I needed right now.

But she wasn't my wife.

FIFTY
EMERY

FOR THE LAST TEN MONTHS, I'd avoided leaving Vermont. I wanted to stick close to home; it just felt like the right thing for me. I spent as much time with Tommy as I could, getting my head in the best place it could be, trying to learn how to live without Jesse.

Since that meant I hadn't been going to Boston, I'd sent Charlotte on my behalf. She would take pictures while she was there, and we would video-chat from the jobsite.

But I really needed to be there in person.

I needed to put my eyes on the construction and make sure it was everything I wanted it to be.

This was my building after all, and I'd lost sight of that to where it no longer meant anything to me.

That wasn't the case anymore.

Charlotte booked us a private plane, and after dropping Tommy off at school, where he'd be picked up by his grandmother and stay the next two nights at her house, we got on board the jet. Once the plane landed, an SUV pulled onto the runway, and we got into the backseat, having the driver take us straight to the jobsite.

I'd been thinking about this trip for a long time, remembering what the city had looked like when I last saw it. That was the night before Jesse died, when Charlotte and I had taken a late flight back to Burlington.

It didn't look like anything had changed while I was gone.

Except for me.

"Are you ready for this?" Charlotte asked as though she were inside my head.

I looked across the backseat. Her phone was on her lap, hands holding it, but her stare was locked with mine.

"I've put it off long enough."

She smiled. It was always so warm. "But are you ready for it?"

I glanced past her, seeing how close we were to the jobsite. And then I took a deep breath and really thought about her question. "Yeah, I think I'm ready."

She turned her body toward me, and with the softest voice, she said, "Boston's skyline is never going to be the same."

I felt myself smile. "That might be true someday soon, but we're far from being done."

"I can still be proud of you."

"Of us," I corrected her. "We did this together, Charlotte."

Her grin dimmed when she saw we were at the construction entrance, and the SUV parked along the curb.

So did mine because, for the several minutes I'd been sharing this space with her, I'd forgotten what today was really about. I'd left my son for the first time since he lost his mother.

More importantly, it was the ten-month anniversary of Jesse's death.

I'd forgotten because of Charlotte.

I sighed as I glanced out my window, and what brought me right back was the feel of her hand on my knee.

"I have a feeling today is going to be amazing," she said as I looked at her again.

Her touch was light and only lasted a second before her fingers were off me. But she was still giving me that smile ... and I felt it everywhere.

We didn't return to my townhouse until after eight o'clock that night. Marion was long gone for the evening, but she had left dinner in the fridge, and she'd put Charlotte's suitcase in the foyer after the driver dropped it off.

Since Charlotte was staying at the hotel down the street, she came inside to grab her bag and was walking toward me with it as I stood in front of the door. "You can say I'm right anytime now, you know." She smirked when she was halfway to me.

She was wearing the same grin from earlier. The one that had distracted me from the thoughts that were torturing my mind.

The grin was doing the same thing to me again right now.

I didn't want to say good-bye just yet.

"Stay." I lifted my hand, gripping the top of the door to stop her from going anywhere. "Marion made enough for the both of us, and I know you have to be starving. We haven't eaten anything all day."

I hadn't checked the fridge, nor had I left Marion any instructions. But she always made several plates of food, and if she didn't, I'd share the one she'd made me if that meant more time with Charlotte.

"I am pretty hungry." Her fingers were still clinging to the handle of the suitcase. "So, I guess I'll have dinner with you."

I told her to hold on a second, and I went outside, handing the driver two twenties from my wallet. "Thanks for waiting," I said to him, "but she's not going to need a ride." Once he took the money, I went back in.

"Let's eat," I said to her, and she left her suitcase and followed me into the kitchen.

When I saw her head for the fridge, I pointed at the barstools. "Sit."

"I'll heat up—"

"Sit, Charlotte. I've got this."

She laughed as she put her hands in the air, making her way over to the stools.

I'd never gotten to take care of Jesse. She always did this part. It'd worked; it was what we'd both wanted. I wouldn't change a thing, and I didn't think she would have either.

But this was different.

I was different ... now.

"You take such good care of me," I said as I stuck the first plate into the microwave. I glanced at her, watching the heat spread across her cheeks. I moved over to the fridge and grabbed a bottle of white wine, holding the automatic opener over the cork. "Maybe I want to take care of you for once." Once the glass was filled, I pushed it toward her.

"Thank you." Her hand wrapped around the stem. "Santa Margherita is my favorite."

I had known that. I'd heard her order it enough times during our trips to Boston, so I'd asked Marion to buy a few bottles.

I turned to take the plate out of the microwave, and I set it in front of her, eventually adding mine to the island once the food was warm. Then, I took the spot next to her with a beer in my hand.

"I think we should toast," she said.

I was quiet for a few seconds. "Can I start?"

She nodded.

"I want to thank you because you're the reason I'm in this kitchen right now. You gave me time to get myself right again by handling things at home and at work. You made sure Tommy, Viv, and I always had everything we needed." I sighed. God, I couldn't believe how hard this was for me. "And you still haven't left me." I clinked my glass against hers. "To you, Charlotte. For saving me."

She took her time studying my face, and when she finally spoke, it was with a different tone, "I would do anything for you and your kids."

She'd been proving that since the police came to the door.

Day after day.

She hadn't left my side. Even now, all these months later, I still had to force her to go home.

I wanted her to know it meant something.

Not just as her boss.

But as someone who cared about her.

I got on my feet and held out my hand to her. "Come here."

She set her fingers on mine, and I pulled her up. With her

standing so close, I could feel the differences between her and Jesse.

There was an inch or two in their height, their hair wasn't the same shade, and Charlotte's eyes were a deep brown where Jesse's were blue.

That was a relief.

I gripped her waist but didn't move. I needed to get used to the feel of her first. The soft sounds she made. Her breathing.

I was taking her all in.

And, because I could feel every one of her exhales, I knew she was doing the same.

"Charlotte," I whispered across her neck as she tilted her face. "You feel so good, so right."

My hands tightened as I ran them up her sides and back down, getting comfortable with all these new curves. Her body was starting to respond, and so was mine.

I found her face, cupping her cheeks. "This is"—I shook my head, unsure of why I had to say this, but something was forcing it out—"all new to me."

There was honesty and adoration in her eyes when she replied, "Me, too. We'll figure it out together."

My lips went to her forehead, and I kissed the center of it, slowly moving down her cheek and across her nose before I hovered in front of her mouth.

"Emery," she whispered as my hand went to her back, and I pulled her in closer.

The sound of her couldn't be more different.

I needed that.

I grazed the edge of her mouth with my lips.

"*Yesss*," she moaned, sending me the sweetness of her smell.

I filled my lungs with it and closed my eyes.
I led her the rest of the way in.
And then I kissed Charlotte Scott.

FIFTY-ONE
CHARLOTTE

ONE OF THE biggest things Charlotte had learned from her boss's wife was the importance of time. Jesse had spoken about it often, and she'd listened. Before Charlotte had met Jesse, time wasn't something she'd ever paid attention to. But, now that she had learned its benefits, she based all of her decisions on it.

That was why she'd waited ten months before she encouraged anything to happen between Emery and her. There had been prior situations where she could have put her hands on him, but the timing hadn't been good.

Last night felt perfect, and that was why she had slept with him.

The guilt was there.

Every time she thought about it, she'd get nauseous.

She probably always would.

But, in Charlotte's heart, she knew she was doing the right thing.

She still believed that when the driver pulled up to

Emery's house, his place being closest to the Burlington Airport.

With his hand on her thigh, they turned down his street, and he looked at her and said, "Tommy's at school. We can take a long shower together and have some breakfast and then get to work."

It killed Charlotte to decline the invite. She wanted nothing more than to step into his massive shower and coat his incredibly sexy body with soap. But, with today being trash day, there was something she really needed to do at home.

"I can't," she said reluctantly. "It's not that I don't want to. I do more than anything, I promise. I just have an errand I have to run before it's too late and I miss the window."

Emery reached forward, brushing his fingers against the side of her cheek. "I'll see you later."

Charlotte watched him get out of the car and walk up to the door. Once he used his code to get in, the driver pulled away. It broke her heart to send him in there alone. This was his first trip; it couldn't have been easy, and she wanted so badly to keep comforting him.

But, now that there was a chance he could come to her apartment, there were a few things she needed to purge before she forgot and it was too late.

The driver pulled out of the Blacks' street and took the same route Jesse had ridden the day she died. He wouldn't be going past the exact spot, but Charlotte drove by it often. Viv and Tommy had tied a bouquet of flowers on the guardrail a few days after the funeral.

Not even the dried-up stems or the twine had survived winter.

But the dent where Jesse's bike had hit the metal was still

there. And, for a long time, before the first dusting of snow, Charlotte could see the brake marks on the pavement where Jesse had attempted to stop.

Every time she saw it, she'd think of the way her life had changed.

Of timing.

How the only thing she had ever wanted was a family and how she now felt she was so close to having one.

When she was dropped off at her tiny apartment, she wheeled her suitcase into the living room, leaving it somewhere on the rug, and she headed for the large bookshelf under her TV.

Two books sat on a shelf by themselves.

Charlotte pulled them into her hands and set them next to each other on the kitchen table.

The one on the right was really a notebook. Jesse had written *Everything* on the front cover in black Sharpie and had it delivered to Charlotte's apartment the night she accepted the job. Charlotte had read the words Jesse had written inside at least a hundred times. Every list, every request—every month, Charlotte would check off each one.

She could recite it all by heart.

She didn't need the notebook in her house anymore.

The one on the left truly was a book. A story Charlotte loved very much.

After all, it was the novel that had changed her entire life.

But there was no need to have that one here either, so she lifted both into her arms, and she brought them to the sink where she ripped out every single page. When the basin was filled with paper, she set it on fire, watching the sheets spark and flicker and turn to ash.

She scraped up the black soot it'd left behind along with the bindings of each book, and she brought them into her one-car garage, dumping it all into the trash can.

She rolled the canister to the curb and felt the lid loosen. As she took it off to adjust, she caught a glimpse of what was inside. On top of a small bag of trash sat the cover of the notebook. The hardcover of the book was beside it, and as the sun came up, it reflected off the font, making the gold lettering really shine, the title pop.

Charlotte read the title over and over.

The Assistant.

Part of her wanted to reach in, take the book cover out, and save it for the rest of her life. It was a sin to throw away something so special. But Charlotte knew the consequences of getting caught, and she just couldn't take the chance.

She shut the lid and made sure it was on securely.

As she was walking back inside her apartment, she felt a wave of nausea move through her stomach. Sweat beaded across her chest. Her mouth began to water.

She ran into the kitchen and gripped the sides of the sink, still covered in black from her little bonfire, and she threw up Marion's breakfast.

It hit her.

All of it—the reality of what had happened in Boston, the weight of what she had just done. She had been carrying it for so long, but right now, it was too much.

It burned as it came up.

And it burned as she thought about it all.

When her stomach was finally empty, the sobs shattered her chest, hurting her throat as much as the bile.

"Jesse!" she screamed at the sink.

She needed to get that out.

Saying it to something felt better than not saying it at all.

And she hadn't said it out loud, not until this point.

As she continued to say it over and over, she let her nose run, and she let her voice go hoarse.

And then she cut herself off, stopping all the tears. She then put herself in the shower, got dressed, and drove to Emery's.

She walked into his office, where he was sitting at his desk, like she hadn't shed a tear all morning.

Like she was ready to conquer whatever he threw at her.

And she did.

EPILOGUE

EMERY - FIVE YEARS LATER

JUST AS I was walking into our bedroom—a mug of tea in one hand, a piece of my wife's favorite lemon pound cake in the other—someone rang our doorbell. Charlotte was several feet away from me, on the floor, busy and unable to answer it. So, I set my mug and dessert on a table in the sitting area and rushed down the long set of stairs to the first floor of the brownstone.

The monitor by the entrance showed it was Alicia, my best friend's wife. Since Charlotte and I had moved to Boston full-time and they were still in Burlington, I didn't see Dennis and Alicia as much. But they owned a condo at 3 Stuart Street, the high-rise I'd built in the Back Bay, and stayed there once a month. This visit, they were celebrating the sale of their home in Vermont, downsizing to a smaller house on the same street.

"Alicia, hi," I said as I opened the door. I moved down the steps to greet her, kissing her on the cheek. When I pulled away, I scanned the sidewalk for Dennis. "Where's the husband?"

She smiled, but it wasn't the grin I was used to.

"You just get me today." She was holding something against her chest and showed me it was a book. "When I was packing up the house, I came across this. Jesse had given this to me to read before Charlotte came to work for you. I'd forgotten I even had it."

I took it from her, checking out the cover. It was worn and brown. *Tumbling Down* was the title.

"I didn't know if you'd want it or not," she said, "but I figured you might be able to do something good with it."

I held the book against my side, processing her choice of words. "I'll put it in our library upstairs."

Her smile grew, revealing how fake it was. "I think that's a perfect idea."

I reached toward her again, kissing her on the cheek before I climbed the few steps to the door. "We owe you dinner to celebrate the sale of the house. Have Dennis call me later, and we'll get something scheduled."

She was on the sidewalk, taking a step away, but glanced over her shoulder and said, "We'll talk soon, Emery."

I went back inside, thinking about my exchange with Alicia, staring at the book that was resting on my palm.

Something didn't feel right.

As I climbed the stairs, I tried to remember if Jesse had ever mentioned this book. We normally hadn't discussed what she was reading. Like Charlotte, Jesse always had a paperback or her tablet in her hands.

Not a single memory came to me.

When I reached the top of the stairwell, I leaned my back onto the banister and opened the front cover. On the inside jacket was a black stamp that said, *Property of Saint Michael's College Library.*

Saint Michael's College?

That was the library where Charlotte had worked as the director of historical resources before she became my assistant.

Jesse had given this to me to read before Charlotte came to work for you.

My hands began to tremor as my gaze shifted to the title page where an inscription had been written.

An inscription ... in Charlotte's goddamn handwriting.

Jesse,
Have a lifetime of enjoyment with this book.
It's a favorite of mine. Hopefully, now, it will become a favorite of yours.
Best,
Bay Scott

Bay was Charlotte's middle name.

She had been named after the bay in the small town in Florida she was from.

I'd never called her by her middle name.

And, since we'd gotten married, she'd dropped it from her name completely.

Why did Jesse have this book?

From Charlotte's library?

From before Charlotte became my assistant?

I was shaking so badly; I had to hold the book with both hands, so it wouldn't drop.

I needed time to really think about this, to process each layer, because none of it was making any fucking sense.

There were too many pieces.

Too many ... possibilities.

Before I had time to even take a breath, I heard a sound that tore straight through me.

A sound I just didn't need right this second.

"*Daaaddy,*" our two-year-old daughter screeched as she hurried to where I stood.

"Hi, baby." I held out my hand, and her tiny fingers grabbed it. "Come play, Daddy," she said, leading me to the bedroom where her mother was on the floor, hitting buttons on a game Maddy had abandoned.

I'd thought I knew Charlotte better than anyone.

I'd thought she held no secrets from me.

Because I didn't hold a thing back from her.

When we were halfway inside the room, Maddy released my hand and was off to play with a toy that was over by our bathroom.

I stopped, and now, I was only a few paces behind Charlotte.

Frozen.

Wave after wave of shock rippled through me while every scenario played through my head.

"Who was at the door?" she asked.

There was no right way to address this.

Thinking about it wasn't going to clarify anything.

I just needed to ask.

I knelt behind her and dropped the book onto her lap, my face going into her neck so that she couldn't turn her head toward me.

"What's this—" she said and halted as she realized what she was looking at.

I breathed her in.

My wife still smelled so sweet.

Just maybe not as sweet as I had originally thought.

My lips moved below her ear. "Alicia said she found this in her house. Jesse gave it to her years ago ... before you came to work for me." I reached across her to open the cover. I was sure she didn't need the reminder, but I showed her the handwritten note anyway. She said nothing, so I gently turned her, and I waited for her eyes to land on me before I said, "Charlotte—or maybe I should call you Bay ... were you ever going to tell me that you knew my wife?"

ACKNOWLEDGMENTS

Nina Grinstead, each time I think it's going to be easier, and every time, we end up getting in deeper. When I thought I was going to break, you kept me going. You believe in me in ways I can't even wrap my head around. You fight for me. And, since the moment I met you, you've completely changed my life in ways I never thought was ever possible. I love you so much.

Jovana Shirley, this one was so outside our norm, and you held me together, lady. Thank you for being so patient with me; it was what kept me going every day. There isn't a better feeling than knowing my words are in your hands. Like I say at the end of every book, I would never want to do this with anyone but you. Love you.

Hang Le, working with you is a dream. You saw our vision immediately, and what you created is beyond anything I ever imagined.

Judy Zweifel, as always, thank you for being *amaaazing*. <3

Nikki Terrill and Andrea Lefkowitz, there aren't enough

words to describe what you mean to me or what you've done for me or what you did for this book. I'm beyond fortunate to have you two amazing women in my life and to call you my friends. Love you so hard.

Kaitie Reister, I love you, girl. You're my biggest cheerleader, and you're such a wonderful friend. Thank you for being you. XO

Crystal Radaker, the last one almost killed us, and this one almost ripped us to shreds. Thank you will literally never be enough. The reason I'm still standing right now is because of you. So much love for you. So, so much.

Kimmi Street, my sister in crime, we're in this together until the end. Like I've said a million times before, you're the sister I never had and the best friend I always wanted. I love us. And I love you.

Ratula Roy, you're my life, and you mean everything to me. I could never, ever do this without you. Love you.

Ricky, my sexyreads, I love you so much.

Donna Cooksley Sanderson, just a few more months until I get to squeeze you. Thank you for everything. Love you. xx

Chanpreet Singh, thank you for always holding me together. XO

Extra-special love goes to Hilary Suppes, Jesse James, Carol Nevarez, Julie Vaden, Elizabeth Kelley, Jennifer Porpora, Pat Mann, Katie Amanatidis, Katy Truscott, my COPA ladies, and my group of Sarasota girls whom I love more than anything. I'm so grateful for all of you.

Mom and Dad, thanks for your unwavering belief in me and your constant encouragement. It means more than you'll ever know.

Brian, my words could never dent the amount of love you give me. Trust me when I say, I love you more.

My Midnighters, you are such a supportive, loving, motivating group. Thanks for being such an inspiration, for holding my hand when I need it, and for always begging for more words. I love you all.

To all the bloggers who read, review, share, post, tweet, Instagram—Thank you, thank you, thank you will never be enough. You do so much for our writing community, and we're so appreciative.

To my readers—I cherish each and every one of you. I'm so grateful for all the love you show my books, for taking the time to reach out to me, and for your passion and enthusiasm. I love, love, love you.

BOOK CLUB QUESTIONS

- Did you think it was fair for Jesse's father to be upset with her for telling her mom about his disease?
- Was it wrong of Charlotte not to tell Emery about her relationship with Jesse, or was honoring her friend's last wishes the right thing to do?
- Do you believe Jesse's death was accidental, or purposeful?
- Is there a book for you, like the teal-and-gold book was for Jesse, that could tell another person about your innermost beliefs and wishes?
- How did it make you feel when Charlotte began to insinuate herself into the lives of Viv, Tommy, and Emery? Did you think she was being manipulative, or a perfect employee?
- If Viv or Tommy end up inheriting the illness, do you believe they'd be more inclined to follow their grandfather's path or their mother's?

BOOK CLUB QUESTIONS

- How would you handle a life-changing diagnosis?
- Would you like the opportunity to hand-pick your partner's next partner, or was that an example of Jesse's micromanagement?

SPOILER GROUP

If you would like to chat about *The Assistant*, click HERE to join the spoiler group.

MARNI'S MIDNIGHTERS

Getting to know my readers is one of my favorite parts about being an author. In Marni's Midnighters, my private Facebook group, we chat about steamy books, sexy and taboo toys, and sensual book boyfriends. Team members also qualify for exclusive giveaways and are the first to receive sneak peeks of the projects I'm currently working on. To join Marni's Midnighters, click HERE.

NEWSLETTER

Would you like to qualify for exclusive giveaways, be notified of new releases, sales, and read free excerpts of my latest work? Then sign up for my newsletter. I promise not to spam you. Click HERE to sign up.

ABOUT THE AUTHOR

USA Today best-selling author Marni Mann knew she was going to be a writer since middle school. While other girls her age were daydreaming about teenage pop stars, Marni was fantasizing about penning her first novel. She crafts sexy, titillating stories that weave together her love of darkness, mystery, passion, and human emotions. A New Englander at heart, she now lives in Sarasota, Florida, with her husband and their two dogs. When she's not nose deep in her laptop, working on her next novel, she's scouring for chocolate, sipping wine, traveling, or devouring fabulous books.

Want to get in touch? Visit me at...
www.marnismann.com
MarniMannBooks@gmail.com

ALSO BY MARNI MANN

STAND-ALONE NOVELS

The Assistant (Contemporary Romance)

When Ashes Fall (Contemporary Romance)

The Unblocked Collection (Erotic Romance)

Wild Aces (Erotic Romance)

Prisoned (Dark Erotic Thriller)

THE AGENCY STAND-ALONE SERIES—Erotic Romance

Signed

Endorsed

Contracted

Negotiated

THE SHADOWS SERIES—Erotic Romance

Seductive Shadows—Book One

Seductive Secrecy—Book Two

THE PRISONED SPIN-OFF DUET—Dark Erotic Thriller

Animal—Book One

Monster—Book Two

THE BAR HARBOR SERIES—New Adult

Pulled Beneath—Book One

Pulled Within—Book Two

THE MEMOIR SERIES—Dark Mainstream Fiction

Memoirs Aren't Fairytales—Book One

Scars from a Memoir—Book Two

NOVELS COWRITTEN WITH GIA RILEY

Lover (Erotic Romance)

Drowning (Contemporary Romance)

Printed in Great Britain
by Amazon